Stillborn Season

Stillborn Season

A Novel

Radhika Oberoi

SPEAKING TIGER

SPEAKING TIGER PUBLISHING PVT. LTD
4381/4, Ansari Road, Daryaganj
New Delhi 110002

Frst published in India by Speaking Tiger in paperback 2018

ISBN: 978-93-87693-92-0
eISBN: 978-93-88070-09-6

10 9 8 7 6 5 4 3 2 1

Printed at Nutech Print Services, India

For Rashmi, my first storyteller, and for Kaushalya,
who took over, *in memoriam*.
For Daisaku Ikeda, Sensei par excellence.

Contents

PROLOGUE

Nagra III

I

Appalling, the lack of manners at the airport. And now, to be jolted about in this dreadful taxi—hardly a fitting welcome for a Goodwill Ambassador, he thought, as he took a seat in the black-and-yellow contraption. The taxi was an Ambassador. The driver—what was his name, Suck-winder—had patted its curvaceous bumper and said, 'Please to step into my *Amby*, sir-ji, it will take you from place-to-place in Dilli, sir-ji.' That had made him laugh, despite his recent irritations.

The interiors of the Ambassador caused him more hilarity, and he almost forgave the Ministry of External Affairs for not sending an official of some sort to receive him at the international arrivals gate of Palam Airport. Panels of thermocol were pasted on the roof—to protect the skull of passengers from cracking open every time the taxi drove over a pothole, he assumed.

'I sticked it,' Suck-winder informed him, when a loose panel grazed his head. 'It makes Amby cool in summer and hot in winter.'

The taxi's dashboard—rough plywood framed with aluminium—was a veritable shrine. Gods and goddesses with multiple limbs and modes of transport—a giant lotus, a tiger—reclined and offered benedictions to whoever gazed at them from the passenger seat, seeking reassurance that the dented, or rather dimpled Leviathan would rattle its way to desired destinations. At the centre of this collection of miniature idols was a framed photograph of an elderly saint, with a saffron turban around his head and a white beard, which seemed as though it would flow out of the frame and onto the dashboard.

'He is my Sache Patshah, sir-ji.' Suck-winder looked into the rear-view mirror and spoke.

'Sa...Sah...what?' the Goodwill Ambassador asked the driver. He was tired; it had been a long flight from London and he wasn't particularly interested in mimicking the local dialect immediately upon arrival.

'Sache Patshah...Guru Nanak...sitting right in the middle of Ma Kali and Ganesh-ji. He is my guru, sir-ji.' Suck-winder smiled as benignly as the guru, who looked unperturbed sliding this way and that with all the other deities whenever the Amby swerved.

'Are you Sikh?' he asked Suck-winder, unnecessarily. The Goodwill Ambassador knew enough about India to tell the difference between Hindus and Sikhs. He had corresponded with the Indian Embassy for months before travelling to New Delhi, to interview the Prime Minister. Letters and books had arrived in London, in brown-paper parcels stamped with the country's recent history—the International Leprosy Congress, the Indo-Soviet Union Manned Space Flight, 100 Years of Postal Life Insurance, the Asiatic Society. But the events that had unfolded in June—when men in olive-green uniforms had marched into the holiest of Sikh shrines with their shoes on, when they had shattered the peace of the sanctum sanctorum with Kalashnikov rifles—would, perhaps, never be commemorated on a one-rupee postage stamp. The Prime Minister had masterminded the attack on the shrine; she had called it an *operation*, executed by the army at her command. The act was *diabolical,* his Indian friends who worked for national dailies had whispered over unclear trunk-call lines.

But he was not here to interrogate her about her misadventures as Prime Minister. He was here, to record on camera, the steely woman who was once a shy young girl, who loved Tibetan bracelets and thought Italy was mouth-watering. He wanted to hear her speak, in her small voice, about her love for words like 'Chimborazo'. He wanted to sit next to her (if she would allow it) in her beige Polara and make her laugh. 'The woman behind the leader of men', 'From dumb doll to public figure'; several catchphrases suggested themselves to him for the profile he was here to shoot, as the taxi rattled through a street clogged with cyclists and motorists trying to outmaneuver what looked like toy cars—Suck-winder said they were the foreign Maruti 800s.

'Only cows can walk unmolested here,' he mumbled, battling a fly hovering precariously close to an eyelash.

'Yes ji, I am a Sikh,' Suck-winder replied, startling the

Goodwill Ambassador who was rolling down a window. 'And you, sir ji...you are?'

The Goodwill Ambassador clapped his pink palms together to crush the fly that was winging its way to his forehead. But it escaped through the window, which he rolled up quickly before turning to Suck-winder. He considered the question. Who was he, really, to this Sikh taxi-driver who had spotted him at the arrivals pick-up point, trying to read the placards—*Welcome Mr Ribert, CEO, Good Leather Expirts; Swagatam Tours and Travels: Swagatam! Mrs Lilly from Leeds; Capital Residency welcomes Mr and Mrs Shelton; Samovar Guest House: Hello! Mr Jacks and Son.* He had not found any with his name on it, not even a misspelt version. And then Suck-winder had appeared amidst the choppy waves of names, and had steered him towards his black-and-yellow Amby. For Suck-winder, the Goodwill Ambassador knew, he was but a foreigner, wretched but rich, a firang who could be charged with a complete disregard for the taxi's fare meter, which he suspected had not even been pushed down to 0.00 rupees.

He wanted to tell this turbaned thug that his mother's father was French, but his mother's father's mother was Italian; his father's mother was Swiss, but his father's mother's mother was Ethiopian. He wanted Suck-winder to know that back home, he was called the best-bred mongrel in Europe, that Bette Davis, her face like cream souring rapidly under a Delhi sun, had once squawked: 'You perfectly foul French upstart!'

'I am from London,' was all he said to the face in the rear-view mirror, which looked like the cracked brown landscape of a BBC documentary on a drought in the Third World.

'Most passengers in my Amby are Angrez or Amrikan,' Suck-winder replied, nimbly rotating the steering wheel with bushy forearms to avoid a Maruti 800 that had jumped a red light. 'This is inter-nation Amby.'

The firang in the back seat flashed his Goodwill Ambassador smile in an effort to look impressed. This smile—an incomplete curve on his face, always unsure about whether to broaden or not—had facilitated many friendships in the past. He had played ping-pong with children in Egypt. He had jabbed needles into the upturned bottoms of Chinese infants, who didn't squeal or wriggle out of his arms, anaesthetized as they were by the mirth on his lips. He had bicycled on dirt tracks in Kenya with truant schoolboys. His benign crescent had lit up wretched streets and shanty towns, like a naked bulb.

The only time it had almost been snuffed out was moments before Suck-winder's turbaned head had appeared in the crowd of placard-bearers. The officer at the immigrations desk had examined his documents, adjusted the square, plastic rim of his spectacles, and bared his teeth. This was his Immigrations Officer smile, the Goodwill Ambassador had thought. Uneven teeth hanging from fleshy gums, flecked with red. Reddish liquid had oozed to the corners of his mouth and he had wiped it with a yellowing-white shirt sleeve before speaking to him.

'You have no visa, Mr U.S. tin-ooov. Go back to England, okay please?' the officer had said, between bouts of chewing something that sprayed more red liquid onto his lips.

The Goodwill Ambassador had summoned the kindliest crescent his lips could form, and had said, 'But the United Nations allows to me to travel wherever I please.'

The immigrations officer had looked up and met the Goodwill Ambassador's smile with his own jagged line of stained teeth. He had examined the documents all over again, first by readjusting his spectacles, which had slipped down the bridge of his nose, and then, by licking his thumb and applying the spit to the corner of each official paper, before turning it over. Finally, after bouts of thumb-wetting and paper-shuffling, he had found a certificate issued by the United Nations, claiming that the foreigner standing in front of him was indeed an international emissary.

The barricades had swung open, and the Goodwill Ambassador had found himself standing in the mild chill of an October morning. Clearly, the Ministry of External Affairs had not been informed about his arrival. Or perhaps the government department was inside an Ambassador which was forced to stop in the middle of the road because a cow was ambling through traffic, trying to get to the other side of the road. Maybe the ministry would never make it to the airport.

He wondered how long it would be before his Amby made it to the hotel.

'Just one more red light, sir ji… Then Sukhwinder will make Amby fly. Your hotel in Chanakyapuri, sir ji… No red lights there.'

Or cows, he dared to hope.

II

Flailing arms reached out, trying to touch her face. Garlands of marigold, and strings of jasmine intertwined with roses were flung at the dais on which she stood. She caught a few of them, and allowed the rest to fall on the makeshift platform. The Goodwill Ambassador sat in a far corner of the dais, observing the Prime Minister as she greeted the crowd at the pre-election rally with her hands joined in a customary namaste. He was unnerved by her seeming disregard for security. Men in dark suits spoke into walkie-talkies as they hovered around her, like a cloud gathering strength as the multitudes that had arrived at the rally swelled beyond the flimsy wooden barricades. A few men in white kurtas and caps shaped like upturned paper boats climbed onto the wooden fencing, which demarcated the stage from the rally grounds. The cumulonimbus of walkie-talkies tightened around her but she emerged from a gap like a thunderbolt. She let them garland her, clutching the end of her handloom sari, which draped her head and fell across her shoulder.

The Goodwill Ambassador felt absurd, sitting on a steel folding chair, facing the restless masses of this eastern state. He had arrived at his hotel in Delhi's Chanakyapuri only yesterday, but before he could slip between the starched white bed sheets of the teakwood double bed, a telephone call had informed him of a change in the Prime Minister's itinerary. The person at the other end of the cherry-red telephone receiver had said, 'A very good afternoon, Mr Pete…umm…Mr Pete… Uss-tin-tin-umm—Mr Pete sir!'

'A very good afternoon to you too,' he had said encouragingly, his fingers tightening around the grooves of the spiral telephone wire. His patience and goodwill had worn off with each jolt that had traumatized him in Suck-winder's Amby, but he wanted to sound cordial, at least till he had interviewed the Prime Minister.

'The Prime Minister will fly tomorrow, Mr Pete sir. You will fly with her?'

A statement with an interrogative inflection. He would have to get used to it. 'Yes,' he had spoken into the mouthpiece, 'I will fly with her.'

He had managed to speak with her on the flight, but only very briefly. Officials in safari suits had flanked them, interrupting their conversation with matters pertaining to the imminent rally, which required her immediate attention. Despite the frequent intrusions, he had softened her steely reserve. Her thin, resolute lips had parted with rare mirth when he had asked her if she preferred being air-borne or earth-bound.

'I used to walk and run on my toes as a teenager, particularly in Nainital or Mussoorie, so I'm used to being air-borne, I suppose,' she had confided.

'And do you visit those hill towns often?' he had asked.

'Not as often as I would like to…as a girl I loved the hills… but there is precious little time for indulgent holidays now,' she had revealed, her voice unusually wistful.

And he had arrived here this morning, in the midst of this heaving, dusty campaign trail. His face felt flushed; he was certain it had disintegrated into blotches of pink and grey. A Bay of Bengal breeze dampened the crisp October morning; it carried with it the betel-nut-and-tobacco-flake breath of the millions who stood on the grounds, holding aloft banners, hollering, 'Bharat Mata ki jai!'

Did they walk to this rally from villages along the coastline? Would the conical loudspeakers, jutting out from a mesh of wires on electric poles, carry her thin voice to these multitudes sitting cross-legged on the uneven ground with its patches of grass and mounds of faeces, cracked dry by the sun? Were they paid a few rupees by those men in capsized-boat caps, to fill the space between the wooden fencing with their slogans, their flags—printed with the ruling party's insignia—their devout attention? Would the soporific drug of her speech lull them into forgetting a summer massacre? The Goodwill Ambassador wondered how much longer he would have to sit on the dais. He would have preferred to be part of the audience, to squat like them in the dirt than to be scrutinized by a swarm of dark eyes, shielded from the October sun by ancient, knotty fingers.

Marigold garlands covered the Prime Minister's neck and shrouded her mouth as she clutched the tall stem of the microphone. The flowers would choke her, he thought—the petals would tickle her small, tight mouth. But the crowd was captivated when the microphone came alive with static.

'Namaskar, bhaiyon aur behnon…' said the Prime Minister, her voice a steady drone, unperturbed by declamatory changes in tone.

'Bhaiyon aur behnon,' she repeated. Her countrymen were her brothers and sisters. The crowd felt compelled to return her greetings.

'Bharat mata ki jai!' chanted the squatters, the betel-nut chewers, the banner-holders, the rally-fillers.

III

Vampire roots swung from the branches of an ancient banyan, almost touching his face. He felt the morning sun trying to filter through the latticework of branch and leaf, but a fog had frozen its rays, and only the cold seeped in through the gaps. The Goodwill Ambassador wanted a cup of tea. The last day of October had sent shivers down the rows of gigantic dahlias that fringed the lawns of the Prime Minister's official residence. And while his resilience to Delhi's sudden but tenacious winter seemed far greater than that of the delicate patchwork of flora that surrounded him, a cup of tea—perhaps a dark Nilgiri—might spread its brisk flavour through his veins and prepare him for the impending interview.

He had researched quite thoroughly. In the months before arriving here, he had ruminated over correspondences between a young girl and her father, who was in prison. He had read her speeches. He had studied black-and-white photographs from her childhood—sitting on a rock under a tree and posing angrily with a doll in her hands, standing against a gauze curtain, her dark ringlets held together by a large bow on one side of her head—and all the other official paraphernalia released by the Indian Embassy. The documents gave him biographical details and a structured timeline of her achievements in office. But they omitted the tumult. They were silent about the unrest. They abbreviated accounts of those policies and measures that had raised the dust of menace at public gatherings. He had sensed it yesterday at the election rally; a fitful throng of vigilant eyes, knotted arms, and mouths contorted with something other than the sycophantic smiles they had flashed as they pelted her with marigold and rose.

The tea, if it arrived, would lend him the strength of a full-leaf brew to coax her into talking about a few impetuous decisions; about a willfulness that made her disregard public opinion. He had not intended to bring up politics during the conversation they were about to have under the banyan tree, in a few moments. He wanted the girl, who once attended St Mary's Convent in a small town by the Ganges, to speak. He had hoped that the frail young woman who had read *The French Revolution: a History. In Three Volumes* and *Joan of Arc: Stories*—both titles had glimmered at him from a bookshelf in her study—would perhaps dwell on philology, and the annoyance wrought by missing eight-letter words in the morning crossword. But the woman who had stood on the rickety dais yesterday, waving to the people, *her* people, who adored and despised her in equal measure, would remain a mere apparition in the interview he was here to film, if he omitted to question her about her political ambitions.

The Goodwill Ambassador shifted in the wicker chair he was sitting on; a tea cosy had appeared in his line of vision. It sat squarely on a tray which was held aloft by a liveried bearer. The tea cosy made its way through a garden path with Ashoka trees on either side. He stopped himself from walking up to meet the bearer halfway; to do so would be to let slip his annoyance at this delayed gesture of hospitality.

But he was accustomed to delays by now. Even here, in the Prime Minister's garden, the local camera crew dispatched by the country's only news channel to film the interview was taking much too long to set up. A sound technician fiddled with the spools and knobs of a Nagra III tape recorder; the machine, wedged between the twigs of a golden duranta hedge, spat to confirm its electromagnetic preparedness for the interview. Two Arriflex cameras stood behind the two wicker chairs under the banyan tree—one on which he sat, and the other, cushioned but empty, lying in wait for the Prime Minister. Cables meandered through concentric formations of gerberas and pansies, strangulating them.

When the local crew had arrived half an hour late, he had instructed the technicians to set up the lights and cameras speedily, but with as much care and courtesy as they could extend to the staff, flora and other live creatures who had made the Prime Minister's bungalow their own. He didn't want to upset her, because a trolley had accidentally flattened a row of poppies.

But the Prime Minister, like the tea, seemed indefinitely delayed. The tea-cosy carrier, who, until a few moments ago, was making his way through the Ashoka-pillared garden path, had turned around, and was walking away from the banyan. The Goodwill Ambassador narrowed his eyes and leaned over the wicker chair for one last look at the bearer who was dwindling rapidly into a speck.

'Maybe teapot is cracked, sahib?' suggested the sound technician, standing beside the Nagra III.

Maybe. Maybe the teapot was empty. Maybe the cups and saucers didn't match. Maybe the sound technician knew more about tea than he did about audio recorders: the circuit board of the Nagra III was like a miniature city, alive with lights. Maybe the Nagra III was recording his consternation, maybe he should instruct the crew to pack up...

There was a loud noise, flat, more like a crack than a boom, with a hint of metal.

'Firecrackers.'

The sound technician was all-knowing. 'Don't worry sahib, it is only children playing with firecrackers before Diwali.'

Another noise. Maybe a firecracker that burst into a conflagration, before it could cascade in twirls of light and colour. Another. A march-past of metal. A blazing standing salute. Then, silence.

'The Prime Minister has been shot,' said someone. Not the sound technician, who looked unsure for the first time since his arrival in the garden. Somebody else. Maybe, a crew member, maybe a bearer...

'Don't move!' The command came swiftly from behind the golden duranta hedge, from the branches inhabited by the colony of bats, from the wicker chairs, the grass. It stilled the garden. The camera crew stood with its arms and legs frozen around tripods, boom poles and microphones. Rows of snapdragon stood vigilant to the movement of bees, grasshoppers and butterflies. The leaves of the banyan didn't sway to a persistent wind causing jitters in an empty sky, although the Goodwill Ambassador thought he could sense their veins grow taut and distended.

The garden was surrounded by people in uniform. Men with rifles emerged from the foliage, taking aim at axils, stamens and internodes. Trees, shrubs, equipment, chairs and the lily pond were cordoned off.

The Goodwill Ambassador held his bundle of pages, wondering if he could still do his piece-to-camera. Nothing stirred, expect the spools of the Nagra III. The sound technician had forgotten to switch it off.

BOOK I

The Assistant Professor

I

Charcoal grey. The colour was fittingly sombre, although Sukant would have preferred a cobalt blue or even a plum red, which reflected his recently acquired taste in Merlot wines. But to dress flamboyantly would be unwise, at least for now. He didn't want his male colleagues at the university's Faculty of English—who wore, with uniform predictability, white kurtas that hung loosely over blue jeans—to think he was a dandified Nehruvian. The jacket was an indulgence he hoped the faculty would forgive him for, after it had collectively raised its eyebrows at the snug contours and the mandarin collar that was left unbuttoned to reveal the crisply ironed shirt underneath. It didn't detract from his abilities to teach *The Prologue to the Canterbury Tales* to a class of distracted undergraduates. But he wondered now, as he stood in front of a full-length mirror in his tiny room, if his seniors would consider him less serious about Chaucer than he was about his appearance. The mirror confirmed his serious-mindedness by reflecting the thin lines that formed on his forehead and around his eyes whenever he frowned—which he did, now. He nodded slightly, and the image in the mirror nodded back at him, in silent agreement that the person in the charcoal-grey Nehru jacket and navy-blue trousers was finally ready to catch the bus to Delhi University's North Campus.

Sukant knew that there had been long whisper sessions among the faculty members in the staff room, in the intervals between classes. Unkind remarks had been made about his thesis, the one he had brooded over the many cold summers spent confined within the neo-Gothic precincts of Cambridge.

'Nationalism in Anglo-Irish Literature,' he overheard them smirking. 'Fancy-pants has an opinion on *nationalism,* and can cite from sources to prove his point.'

'And earn his pint,' said a tea-slurping elder.

'And entertain a lass, over a joint,' said another in glee.

He ignored them. If *they* were that full of nationalistic fervour, they should change the syllabus, he thought. They should replace grassy meadows and daffodils with parched lands and chamelis. Cathedrals with temples, and maybe a mosque or two. Bonnets with dupattas, governesses with Adivasi ayahs, abused and exploited by the families whose meals they cooked and toilets they cleaned.

Despite the derision and the relentless staring he faced in the staff room every day, Sukant was glad that he was back to teach in a country where he had been taught in his undergraduate years, when the glimmer of western shores had been a vague and distant possibility. At Cambridge, cycling down streets that forked into slivers only to converge at intersections that tinkled with tearoom china, he had missed the dust of the faraway lanes of his youth. He had longed for drowsy afternoons spent in a sticky heat, which was quelled by the khus-scented air of a giant cooler. Watching the punters on River Cam, he had summoned from memory those ancient fishing boats that slithered over the waters of the Hooghly.

This was Delhi, not Calcutta, he reminded himself, as he collected a stack of marked assignments and put them in his jute-and-cloth jhola. And though he was back in his own country, he was still far away from home. It was all a temporary arrangement: the teaching position in a college in North Campus, this room on the terrace of a house in a South Delhi neighbourhood where he was writing his first novel, the bone-rattling bus rides to the university, his landlord's insistence that he use water and electricity and gas sparingly to 'preserve the energies of our country'. He would have to live as comfortably as was possible within the strained means of a lecturer's salary, until his book was published and his debut declared 'dazzling' in gushy reviews. Maybe then, after his eagerly anticipated launch into the world of fiction, he could quit his job and move to Calcutta to write full-time.

He smiled encouragingly at the image in the mirror, whose daily routine was frequently interrupted by the onset of fantasy. He was getting late; maybe the bus had already left. He glanced at his bed. Anita was stirring in her sleep. He could see the undulating curves of her body underneath the bed sheet. If the bus had left, maybe he could peel off the jacket and spend the rest of the day under the sheet too.

Anita. He hoped *she* was not a temporary arrangement. She was what made Delhi feel like a pleasurable stopover on the path to literary fame. It was because of her that this rented hole in the wall felt like glamorous poverty—a pre-requisite to making literature that would endure and even outlive the fashions of the day. Her eau de cologne gave the sweat of her armpits a citrus tang; her chiffon sari lent the garret the grace and mystery of a boudoir. She wafted in and out of the cramped space, draped in lavender or powder blue, the paper-thin fabric rustling against Sukant's skin as he removed the safety pins and undid the pleats that held it all together.

He wondered if he should wake her up. She couldn't be here, in his bed, while he was at the university. The landlord, Ranbir Chawla, would combust with self-righteous rage. He knew that Sukant had a 'lady friend' who made 'visitations' but he had made it very clear to Sukant that the lady friend 'must not do night spend'. She would do day spend then, Sukant had thought, but had nodded his compliance to the landlord's code of behaviour for 'educated baba log'. He would have to find a way to get her out of the room—perhaps they could sneak out through the narrow, winding staircase that clung to a wall at the rear of the house, leading to the servants' quarters. To use the main staircase would be risky now; Ranbir Chawla was probably returning from his brief morning walk and lengthy gossip session with other elderly householders in the neighbourhood park. It wouldn't do to upset his fragile nerves, calmed by a bout of breathing exercises, with an early-morning sighting of a girl in crumpled chiffon.

II

A cloud of smoke cleared to reveal the contours of a bus. It gasped to a halt at the stop, as though to catch its rusty-engine breath, and lurched ahead almost immediately after a few passengers had jumped onto the footboard. Sukant chased the vehicle before it slowed down and he clambered in, his body hauled up by the outstretched arms of the bus conductor.

He reached the university in time for his class, and found his students huddled around a transistor. Its antenna was pulled up to its full height. Probably to catch a song from *Utsav.* How was he going to teach them a sentence of fourteenth-century English literature if all they could think of, and sing by rote, were the songs of a fifth-century courtesan who lived in the city of Ujjain, whose alter ego on the big screen was the red-lipped, big-hipped Rekha. Or maybe there was a cricket match between India and Pakistan, and the students were following the trajectory of the ball through the non-stop commentary.

A boy broke away from the group and walked up to him. Pradeep. A front-row occupant. Studious-looking, with hair neatly parted on the side, his was the sole hand that shot up regularly in class to answer a question or to say something profound that belied his youthful face. It was highly unlikely that he would append himself to a group listening to Hindi songs on Vividh Bharti. Cricket too, Sukant knew, was of little interest to one of the few students in class who knew that the Wife of Bath was not a housewife who went to the city's Gymkhana Club for a swim every day.

'The Prime Minister has been taken to AIIMS, sir,' said Pradeep, his voice low but steady. 'She was shot by her own bodyguards…two Sikh men.'

The other students slowly broke away from the group and converged around Sukant as he stood transfixed to the classroom floor, books in hand.

'Haven't you heard the news, sir?' asked Rahul, whose transistor it was. He increased the volume. Waves of static sizzled through the newsreader's soft voice that informed them that surgeons were trying to remove bullets from the Prime Minister's chest.

Sukant was sickened by the suddenness with which the news had been sprung upon him. He was also ashamed of his self-absorbed oblivion—he had probably been trying on the Nehru jacket when she was shot. The bus had crossed the chaotic AIIMS intersection in the morning but he had not noticed anything unusual about the convoy of white Ambassadors with red beacons flashing urgently, bringing traffic to a halt. He had grumbled about the bureaucracy whooshing across the city in cavalcades that slowed down the lives of people trying to make an honest living. He had enveloped himself in *The Times of India*, doing the crossword before he scanned the headlines, not hearing the menace of sirens around him.

He wondered if he should call off the class. But he could

hear the steady drone of lectures from other rooms. He asked, 'Do you want to go home?'

'Let's finish *The Knight's Tale* today, sir. What's the point of going home now; we're all here.' The voice came from a corner of the classroom, near a window drenched in sunshine. Vikas sat there with one hand on the desk, and the other under it, his fingers interlocked with Saraswati's. They always sat together, the two of them, but the entwined fingers were a recent development, which confirmed what Sukant had suspected for a while. Though they never sat in the front row and sported a general air of scruffy cool—Vikas always wore his t-shirt part tucked in, part hanging out of his imported Pepe jeans, and Saraswati had recently had her hair permed—they were secretly nerdy about literature. Sukant was thrilled that they were unwilling to leave *The Knight's Tale* unfinished, even though the Prime Minister had been shot in the morning.

'Yes, let's finish it,' said Pradeep, his brows furrowing as he took out a notebook and arranged his stationary on the desk. The rest of the class sniggered before following suit and opening their bags to pull out books, flip through pages, or borrow ball-point-pens from neighbouring desks.

Sukant opened a page of his text but couldn't focus on the words. The Prime Minister was probably dying, or dead, killed by Sikhs. There were Sikh students at the university. What if a group on campus turned rowdy and attacked them?

He read a sentence, unsteadily. Would he get home that evening? Would his students?

III

The push and pull to catch the evening buses was more than usual. No one wanted to travel in the dark; there were rumours of shadowy figures lurking on every corner. Sukant was nearly crushed by a crowd pressing its way into the narrow door of the bus that he was trying to get into, but he clutched his books close to his chest, pushed himself ahead, and then flung his entire being—body, books, jhola—into the bus.

It was crammed with passengers, and Sukant, unable to find a seat, stood in the narrow aisle, his body squeezed between other standing passengers. A few hours had changed everything. The everyday banter of commuters who shared the same route to and from North Campus had been replaced by a nervous silence. Earlier that day, news of violence had travelled along the corridors of the college, interrupting classes with cryptic messages of impending doom. The Prime Minister was dead; her body would be taken from AIIMS to Teen Murti Bhavan where it would lie in state; the Sikh President's cavalcade had been pelted with stones as it had made its way to AIIMS; arsonists with kerosene cans were stalking the city. All India Radio had replaced its usual news bulletins with mournful music, and Doordarshan grappled with erratic transmission for which it apologized frequently; but the people knew, long before the official declaration, that their Prime Minister was dead.

The bus would have to cross the AIIMS intersection. Sukant felt his muscles grow tense at the thought of travelling through an area seething with anger. He looked around, trying to identify troublemakers. Almost immediately, a few furtive glances were thrown at him. The assassination had turned everyone into a possible pelter of stones, or a murderer. The silence in the bus was oppressive, broken occasionally by the shuffle of feet, or a briefcase rattling against a seat. Each sound was amplified by the fear of what might happen at the next red light or around the next corner—it widened terrified eyes and froze faces into a shocked 'O'.

Sukant wondered whether his students had made their way to safety through treacherous streets. Vikas had a motorcycle, and Saraswati was probably with him, pillion-riding in the twilight. He had instructed them to get home before dark, and to avoid detours or shortcuts. The rest of the class was probably in some bus or the other, like him, and he hoped there would be no rioting as they traversed different routes across the capital. He would call as many of them as possible once he was home. They had stayed back for the class; they had completed *The Knight's Tale* even though the assassination, and the distant rumbling of the mayhem it had unleashed, had destroyed the peace and certainty of hours regimented by a timetable.

The doubts he had managed to quell, about his return from Cambridge, resurfaced now in the form of a migraine. Had he been a sentimental fool to return to this country, where violence, like a sudden flood tearing open an embankment and drowning an entire village, could mangle an ordinary day and the lives of all those who woke up to it?

The bus slowed and a few people boarded it, swelling the crowd in the narrow aisle. One of them, a lanky Sikh teenager in a blue patka, eyed the crowd somewhat shiftily. Sukant sensed a change in the mood of his co-passengers, from vague anxiety to palpable dread. A few of them were staring at the boy as though he was responsible for the murder of the Prime Minister. How unfair was this? What had come over this city for it to look upon a boy with such hostility? Sukant felt like touching his shoulder and asking him what his name was, where he lived, where he was going in a bus full of deranged people. And why wasn't he home already.

'Get down,' someone hissed.

Sukant turned around. A passenger had grabbed the boy and was pushing him down. Were they going to kill him inside the moving bus?

'What are you doing? Leave the boy alone,' Sukant managed to say, his voice a pathetic bleat.

The man holding the Sikh boy tightened his grip, and stared at Sukant with eyes whose irises seemed to have disappeared. Dirty white flecked with red. Other passengers too, were looking at him with the blankness of psychopaths on a mission. The Sikh was going to die, and so was he. He considered jumping out of the moving bus.

'Here…under this,' said the man to the teenager, and pushed him in the space underneath a seat.

Sukant realized that they were crossing AIIMS. He saw a few people running alongside the bus. They are probably trying to get on, he thought. Would it slow down to let them climb the footboard? Should he get out of the vehicle the moment it did?

'Any Sikhs inside?' said one of the men, running parallel to the bus, addressing himself to a passenger sitting by an open window.

'No,' said the passenger quickly, not looking outside.

'Koi Sikh passenger hai to bolo,' said another man, also chasing the bus. He spoke with the matter-of-factness of a conductor punching tickets.

'No,' said someone else, from inside the bus.

'No,' repeated other passengers, picking up the refrain.

'No Sikh passengers on Bus 47,' said the conductor, peeping out of a window briefly.

Sukant managed to peek at the men through a crack in the jostle of heads and shoulders in the aisle. They were carrying kerosene cans and iron rods. He realized, belatedly, that they were not office-goers who had arrived late at the bus stop. They were the stony faces of a crazed mob.

The men, tilting their necks to get a better view of all the passengers, stopped running alongside the bus once they had looked at everyone. It picked up speed.

The boy crouching under the passenger seat blinked a few times, his head sticking out between the trousered legs of the man who had pushed him down, and who now sat above him.

Too dazed to know how lucky he is, thought Sukant, ashamed of his outburst. His eyes grew moist. Mortified by the appearance of tears, he turned sideways for a glimpse of the road that heaved with traffic and bore no sign of the horrors that loomed at crowded intersections. He *was* a sentimental fool, who no longer doubted his decision to return from Cambridge to this country, where the sudden ticking of violence was diffused by a bus full of quick-thinking strangers.

IV

Anita was waiting for him, slumped on the dark staircase outside his door, when he got to his room later that evening.

'You shouldn't be here,' he said, holding her.

He had carried her down the stairs that morning, half-asleep, and had managed to put her in a rickshaw before Ranbir Chawla had reached home. He had worried about her on the way to the university; Anita was as indolent as she was bright. She taught landscape architecture at the School of Urban Planning, and Sukant had fretted over her spending the day in her working women's hostel, in a haze of hash and camaraderie with other working women who had taken the day off.

Now, he was preoccupied with thoughts of his students, of Ranbir Chawla lurking outside his room, of the terms and conditions of his tenancy agreement.

'Relax, he knows I'm here. He didn't give me the spare key, the senile old bag, said he couldn't find it, haha...we were all obsessing about you,' she said. 'I called the uni but the phone just rang and rang,' she continued, wiping the sweat off his forehead with her sari pallu. 'Then someone came on the line, I think it was a guard, and when I asked about you, he said "Sukant sahib gone!" Sukant sahib *gone*? "Where did he go?" I asked him. He didn't know. You know, all hell broke loose near AIIMS…your bus route…I was sick with worry…'

'I'm home now,' said Sukant, a bit obviously, in the 'teacher-preacher tone' he knew irritated her. He fumbled inside the room and found a diary. He then turned around to walk out.

'Where are you going?'

'The students… I have to call them…'

Anita grabbed him by the shoulders. 'Call them later… Look at me first.' She held his face between her palms. They were cold and clammy. 'Ranbir Chawla was saying things could get worse after today. Even the President's convoy was attacked. God knows what they might do next.'

'Nothing will happen…at least not here,' he said.

'You know…that newly married Sikh couple in the barsati a few houses away…what are their names…Gur…Gurpreet and that sweet thing, Kiran?' she asked, lighting a Wills Navy Cut.

'Gursimran and Kiran. They moved here recently,' said Sukant. 'What about them?'

'Yaya… Gursimran and Kiran. It could get bad for them.' She blew smoke at him as she spoke.

'What could get bad for them? Nothing has happened *here*.' Sukant was getting increasingly anxious about his students. He had to call them, now. He didn't know the newlywed couple;

he had only seen Gursimran jog around the neighbourhood park in the mornings. The barsati they lived in was on the terrace of a huge house that Sukant was sure no one could ever break into.

'Ranbir Chawla was saying that if things get worse, if there is a full-scale riot, then their landlord might throw them out. Who would want to risk having Sikh tenants holed up in his barsati?'

'Ranbir Chawla doesn't know a damn thing. He should do some Pranayam and be quiet. He shouldn't go around making a ruckus about things he doesn't really know… Strange that *you* should be chatting with a man who always looks half asleep…'

'I wasn't *chatting* with him, we were *discussing* the situation.' Anita threw the half-finished cigarette on the floor and stubbed it out with a sandalled foot.

'No one knows what the situation really is. All I know is my class was on these crazy streets, trying to get home this evening. All I need to know is whether they got home, or not.' Sukant lit a cigarette and inhaled deeply. He offered it to Anita, to establish a temporary truce.

Kali

I

He squatted on his cabbage patch under the relentless supervision of an early November sun. Major L.D. Budhwar (Retired)—the word was enclosed in parentheses in bold red on the mailbox, as if justifying his gardening in partial nudity to visitors, loiterers and passers-by—examined the leaves of what was to be his evening meal. The cabbage was the star of his cruciferous garden; its spring-green leaves untouched by disease and eager for recruitment to the dining table.

Major Budhwar had fought and won important wars in his vegetable garden. Last year in October, a hailstorm had been averted when he ran out in his striped cotton half-pants, chanting the Gayatri Mantra at a gathering of clouds threatening to destroy a young guava tree. A few hailstones had struck the tree before the storm had relented and shed tears of remorse, allowing it a full lifetime of fruit-bearing. The birds in Major Budhwar's skies—cheels, parrots, crows and pigeons—had been terrorized into changing the trajectory of their flight by a scarecrow he had created: the face of Goddess Kali, with glowering eyes and bloody tongue painted on an overturned earthen pot that hung from a pole in the midst of his nursery. Rats and squirrels had been caught in carefully placed traps, which enticed the offending rodent with slices of bread laced with sedatives.

The garden thrived under the vigilant care of Major Budhwar, rewarding his toil with spectacular root, fruit or leaf, and nourishing his family with home-grown vitamins and minerals.

But it wasn't birds or rodents that threatened the well-being of Major Budhwar's garden. He knew that trouble arrived in a frothy pink frock, every day. Amrit jumped across the wall that separated Major Budhwar's lush vegetation from his neighbour's neatly manicured and characterless lawn. She usually stood in the middle of the cabbage patch, an incongruous blob of pink amidst the thick foliage.

He spotted her now, not in the cabbage patch, but in the tomato shrubbery. He contemplated fumigating her, to eradicate her once and for all. But before he could banish her with his most ferocious, 'Shooo-shooo!' reserved for squirrels, snails and ladybirds, his granddaughter Sweetie bounded out of the house and into his vegetable garden. Together, the girls turned the hallowed furrows into a playground. They murdered sprigs of mint with their clumsy feet, played ball with cabbages, plucked the stillborn fruit of new bushes.

In the five-and-a-half years that it had taken Sweetie to turn into a vegetable-stomping monster, she had not revealed a trace of defiance. This was the influence of Amrit, the child next door, who arrived every day in a new frock and with new tricks to delight Sweetie on this sacred piece of land that was off-limits for children.

II

It wasn't Amrit's fault that she had nothing to do in the winter afternoons that had left a yawning hole in her days. She should have been at school, but many educational institutes in the city had shut down mid-term. Major Budhwar considered asking her grandfather, Jaspreet Singh, when her school would reopen. But he knew that his old friend would not have a definite answer. No one knew anything these days. After the Prime Minister's murder, Jaspreet Singh had disappeared indoors. Major Budhwar had not seen him in the neighbourhood park for the last two or three days. He had abandoned his morning walks in the colony with Major Budhwar and other gregarious septuagenarians, for a brief stroll in the lawn that appended his home.

He's probably watching the news, thought Major Budhwar, making his way to the tomato shrubbery to shoo the girls away. A riot had turned the nip in the air into a premature chill. Many Sikhs had been murdered in South Delhi—shops and houses smouldered in Defence Colony, Safdarjung, Yusuf Sarai and South Extension. And now, if the news was to be believed, rioters and arsonists could torch their beautiful neighbourhood as well.

'This is the time to watch out for murderous vermin,' he muttered, hovering over the girls in his half-pants. Amrit was sitting under the shade provided by tomato shrubs heavy with fruit, building a little stove with crisscrossed twigs. Sweetie was rolling mud balls into tiny chapattis.

'You two...what are you two doing here?' he said, leaning against a neem tree, trying to control his rage.

'Oh-ho Major uncle, can't you see? We are making lunch for the squirrels,' said Amrit, her voice carrying the sting of raw mango with red chili powder on it.

Major Budhwar considered snapping a neem branch and chasing Amrit with it. Instead, he said, 'The squirrels are taking a nap. They are good squirrels; they listen to their parents; they do their homework and when it is finished, they take a nap.'

'No they don't... Look over there, Bade Daddy, that squirrel is climbing a wall...and, over there, that squirrel is eating your grass...and, over there, that squirrel is running after a lizard.' This keen, breathless observation was made by Sweetie, *his little Sweetie*, who was always bolder in Amrit's company.

Major Budhwar mustered all the authority that his relationship with Sweetie allowed him to impose. He was her Bade Daddy, her father's father, the biggest daddy in the household. When he felt dictatorial enough, he said to Sweetie, 'You go in, I say. Go, do your homework... Go, go!'

'But...Bade Daddy,' Sweetie protested, her face contorting and turning red, her eyes narrowing and squeezing out tears, which rolled down her cheeks and splattered on the mud chapatti in her hands.

'And you!' Major Budhwar turned towards Amrit. 'You go back home. Don't you have any homework?'

Amrit, who had flung her arms around her friend the moment she had started to bawl, was now wiping her snotty, mud-stained face with a lace handkerchief that had her initials A.K.—Amrit Kaur—embroidered on it. She looked at Major Budhwar with a defiance he wanted to thrash with the branches of something thorny.

'I have lots and lots of homework, but Dadaji is busy,' she said.

'So? What business has your Dadaji with your homework?' Major Budhwar bristled like his potted cacti.

'Oh-ho Major uncle, said Amrit, her eyes widening at the stupidity of his question. 'Dadaji *does* my homework. My sums. My multiplication tables. And all the *Use the following words in a sentence* exercises, which Joyce Miss has given. He does everything, but he is busy these days.'

This information was not new to Major Budhwar. He knew that Jaspreet Singh could solve math riddles with the ease with which he could recite his beloved Japji Sahib. He knew that his pink-cheeked neighbour, fond doer of primary-school homework, was spoiling his granddaughter rotten.

'I will tell your Dadaji not to do your sums,' threatened Major Budhwar.

'You can't talk to him. I told you he is *very busy*. If you try to talk to him, he only says, "Hmmm" or "Gmmmph".' Amrit mimicked Jaspreet Singh's growly tone with considerable exactitude for a five-year-old.

Sweetie, who had stopped crying and was standing a little behind Amrit, giggled.

'Very busy? What is he very busy with?' Major Budhwar felt tiny beads of sweat erupt on his bare back. Was it the November sun warming his flesh, or was it the warning sign of an impending heart attack brought about by a vegetable assassin?

'Watching TV. He keeps watching TV all day long,' said Amrit.

'Watching TV? What does he watch on TV? *Chitrahaar*?' Major Budhwar sniggered at the thought of old Jaspreet salivating over Rekha and Sridevi and Dimple as they crooned and cavorted around evergreen banyan trees with Amitabh, or that fellow who only wore tight white pants, Jeetendra.

'Oh-ho, Major uncle, maybe *you* watch *Chitrahaar* all day. *My* Dadaji watches an aunty who talks on TV. She wears a flower in her hair. She keeps saying that there is trouble in the city. Dadaji keeps watching her. He ignores me.' Amrit's voice dropped when she spoke the last few words. The child was clearly not used to being ignored.

So Jaspreet is worried, thought Major Budhwar. He was the only one in the family next door who wore a turban, and would immediately be targeted by the rioters, who seemed to know which families were Sikh and which were not, in every neighbourhood around here. To Amrit he said, 'Tell your Dadaji to meet me in the park tomorrow, okay?'

'He won't come outside. Mama and Papa won't let him. They said he will have to remove his pagri and cut his hair if he wants to go out. But Dadaji said no, he will never do that,' Amrit informed him, before squatting on the floor to resume making lunch for the squirrels. Sweetie looked at her grandfather shyly, then sat down cross-legged next to Amrit.

'He won't come outside and you two won't go inside,' hollered Major Budhwar. He finally snapped a tender neem stalk and lunged towards the children with it. 'SHOO-SHOO-SHOO!' he roared, as the girls got up and ran across his patches of cauliflower, trampled his poppies, and broke the long necks of early sunflowers.

'Iff…if you des-troy my gar…garden,' he gasped, running after them, one hand holding up his half-pants that had slipped a few inches from his waist, 'Goddess Kali will…yes…sh…she will des…destroy you!' he managed to shout.

He noticed that Amrit had stopped running when she heard this. He paused as well, flushed and out of breath, a hand on his aching hip.

'No she won't,' said Amrit, pointing at the head of the scarecrow dangling from its pole. 'You know why…You know why…'

'Why?' screamed Major Budhwar, startling a pair of pigeons necking each other on a low-lying branch.

'I know she is not Kali Ma, Major uncle, I know this Kali Ma is just a pot you have painted so badly…and look…look…she doesn't have any hair. How can Kali Ma be bald, Major uncle?'

'SHOO!' he yelled, picking up the stalk of neem and chasing Amrit away.

III

Major Budhwar sensed a disturbance in his vegetable garden just as he was laying his silver-grey head on a spotless white pillow for the night. He was weary with the day's work—trimming the rose bushes, tapping each glossy tomato in the shrubbery to check for firmness, removing ladybirds perched on the leaves of his dahlias and placing them tenderly on the branches of the neem tree instead, shooing the children out of his nursery.

He stumbled out of bed and made his way across the dark garden path to his vegetable patch. He thought he heard a noise—what if rats were burrowing deep into the furrows, nibbling on bulbous roots or on leaves and leaving their droppings on an entire generation of peerless bitter gourd?

He flashed a torchlight on the vegetable patch. Everything looked undisturbed; the vegetables slept peacefully under the moonlit sky. Kali looked magnificent with her piercing eyes and blood-soaked tongue. And the wild locks around her face added to her appearance of murderous rage.

His torchlight lingered on Kali. The locks were long and dark, with a few thick strands of silver running through them. He took a closer look at Kali's face. He thought the eyes of the scarecrow blinked when the light fell on them. The torchlight picked up the shape of something lying between the furrows. An open box of water colours—red, blue, green, ochre in rounded compartments. A wet paintbrush lay dipped in the groove of red paint.

So the girls were here again, he thought, as he brought his face closer to Kali's. The forehead of the scarecrow crinkled up.

Major Budhwar was about to touch the face of Kali, with its wet paint, blinking eyes, and anxious forehead, when he heard a rattling at his gate. He turned around, and saw a group of men standing outside. Their faces were covered with white cloth. They were holding iron rods, and cans of a liquid that Major Budhwar knew was not water.

'Arre uncle,' someone from the group said, in a gentle voice that raised the hair on Major Budhwar's neck and arms. 'The family next door…Sikh family?'

Major Budhwar swallowed before replying, 'No.' He could hear Kali breathe heavily behind him.

'Arre uncle…at your age, why lie, haan?' said the voice from the group, calm and mollifying. 'Come on, we know that one of them, the old man, he wears a pagri… But where is he…he is not at home…is he by any chance hiding here, in your home, haan?'

Major Budhwar's limbs had started to tremble. He leaned against the neem tree before replying, 'There is no one here, but me…and my plants.'

The man who was the voice of the group flashed a light upon the vegetable garden. The light caught the shape of a frail old man in cotton half-pants, standing amidst a furrow of cabbages. The tomato shrubbery jumped out from the dark when the light fell on it. Brinjals revealed themselves, and gigantic dahlias emerged from the shadows.

The light rested on Kali's face. The scarecrow stood stiffly with its arms outstretched, its eyes wide and shining, its scarlet tongue hanging from its mouth, portending death. A gentle breeze lifted its locks of hair. The light detected this movement and lingered on the hair.

Major Budhwar stood transfixed to his cabbage patch for what seemed like an eternity, praying silently to Lord Vishnu, the preserver of the universe, that the cold milkwood-pine scented air would not make Kali sneeze.

The beam of light moved away from Kali and fell on other foliage before it was switched off. The group of rioters started to walk away from Major Budhwar's gate.

When he could no longer see them, Major Budhwar turned around to face Kali. Tears streamed down the face of the old scarecrow, smudging the paint on it.

Tenants

I

The image on the television set was grainy. It disintegrated into waves that settled and formed thin lines, but returned after the country's only news broadcaster flashed an apology on the screen for the recurrent interruptions: 'Rukawat ke liye khed hai'. Even though the picture was blurred, Kiran could see the expression on the face that lay inside the gun carriage. Eyes closed, lips puckered in permanent scorn, forehead creased as though still in deep thought about some unfinished business—a file left unsigned, a bill that would never become an Act of Parliament, a speech that would grow old and meaningless on yellowing sheets of paper.

Kiran slurped her morning tea as she watched the distorted images on the black-and-white Dyanora TV set. The body of the Prime Minister, draped in the tricolour, strewn with rose petals and thick garlands, lay in state at Teen Murti Bhavan. Kiran's eyes moistened when she saw the Prime Minister's grandchildren in the crowd of mourners that surrounded the gun carriage—a bespectacled boy in a starchy white kurta, and a teenage girl, his sister, also in white. The scene was like one from a bad movie, in which the hero dies, or is killed, and the villain survives. But unlike the movies, where a tragic moment is immediately followed by a song-and-dance sequence to ease the tension, this was real life, and the cremation, which would take place in a day or two, Kiran sensed, would be followed by more deaths.

The news—read out by a newscaster whom Kiran both admired and envied, for her skill in addressing the nation without batting an eyelid, and for wearing a new sari each time she appeared on the screen—merely announced incidents of rioting here and there. The latest bulletin had upset Kiran. The riots, which had broken out soon after the Prime Minister was killed, had spread to these parts of the city. *Her* parts of the city, the ones she had grown to love after moving into this barsati with her husband, Gursimran. The tiny room, with its attached kitchen and bathroom, was all they had, a place to start a new life in the capital. Gursimran worked in a bank, and while 'his prospects were bright', as Kiran told the ladies in the neighbourhood, her irises in a swoon whenever she mentioned him, his income was still not enough for them to move to larger and more permanent quarters. The barsati, built as an afterthought by the landlord, Lala Kanshi Chand, to fill the family's substantial coffers with a bit of rental income, was perched on top of his house. It was surrounded by water tanks and a variety of potted plants of medicinal efficacy and ritualistic use. Kiran, who found it hot in summer and gusty in winter, had grown accustomed to its whimsical location that caught the first beams of the morning sun, the twirl of an early fog, or leaves that had fallen off their branches and landed outside the door. Slowly, with Gursimran's frequent and failed attempts to help her cook, or keep the room tidy, she had turned the place into their home.

Kiran had heard about Sikh men being burnt alive in their homes and on the street, by men carrying rubber tyres and cans of kerosene, from Kanta, the landlord's wife, who had received this information from Lala Kanshi Chand, who read the *Times of India* every day. It was whispered, in the local market, that skeletons of charred scooters and motorcycles lay on arterial roads and intersections. The army had taken over Delhi to patrol the streets during morning and evening curfew, said the sabziwala. Dilli has gone mad, said the Chand family khansama, Dilli has no respect for the late Prime Minister, whose last rites have still not been performed, who lies cold in her father's house for all to see and all to weep.

Kiran barely slept in the nights following the Prime Minister's assassination. Once, she had woken up, her nightie damp with sweat, imagining footsteps climbing up the stairway and people breaking into their flimsy room with knives and daggers. She had trembled uncontrollably at the thought of Gursimran, who lay unafraid and fast asleep in her arms, being butchered. They would kill him, she had thought, they would slit his soft throat and set his hair—his messy head of thick hair that she was tangled in—on fire. They would throw a tyre around his neck, set fire to it, and watch him go up in flames. Her quiet sobs had woken her husband, who had pulled her into his arms and said, 'If they break in, they will die. You are safe with me, jaanu.'

Kiran was not convinced that they were safe in the barsati. And she feared that Lala Kanshi Chand, a devout Hindu, would throw them out if the situation worsened after the state funeral. He wouldn't want to risk the welfare of his own family—two married sons and their children who lived on the floors below the barsati—by letting a young and boisterous Sikh couple live in his home.

There was every reason to behave like ideal tenants now, thought Kiran, as she switched off the television set and opened the rickety door of the kitchen to make breakfast for Gursimran. She had been watching the news from the moment Gursimran had left for his routine jog around the neighbourhood park. This was the only time that she could, for, the previous day, he had unplugged the television set and threatened to throw it from the balcony of their barsati into the landlord's garden if she continued to watch images of the Prime Minister's body lying in the garlanded gun carriage—as though she had herself been orphaned. He would be back soon, his face flushed, his body slick with perspiration after the jog. Kiran pushed aside the thoughts that caused a twitch in her lower belly, when she imagined Gursimran running up the winding staircase that led to their room. This was the favourite part of her day, when Gursimran returned from his jog and went into the tiny bathroom for a bath before breakfast.

Kiran usually followed him into the bathroom. But today,

she wouldn't, she said firmly to herself, as she rolled some dough into a ball and flattened it with a rolling pin to make an aloo paratha. She always pretended that the door wasn't latched and that she had walked in by mistake. He always feigned horror at finding her there, in that cramped space with its plastic buckets and leaky taps. He would rush to wrap a towel around his outraged modesty as she grabbed him, uncoiling his hair, running her fingers through it to loosen the knots, soaking his scalp with a mug of hot water. She would then lather his hair with a red chunk of Lifebuoy soap, kneading his scalp like she kneaded a mound of dough—gently here, firmly there. She would scrub the sweat and grime away and wrap his head in a towel. They always emerged from the bathroom separately; he came out first and she a few seconds later, praying silently that Kanta, who was usually lurking on the terrace, hadn't noticed that they had been inside together.

She would let him bathe alone today. Lala Kanshi Chand had complained frequently about taps running dry. Kanta had heard noises, 'like wild elephants taking a bath', when she had stood on the terrace one day, plucking tulsi leaves for her morning puja. If they were asked to vacate the premises now, where would they go, the two of them, in a city baying for the blood of Sikhs?

Through the kitchen window she could see Gursimran standing under a mulberry tree in the park. He always paused to chat with a group of elderly men who converged there after their morning exercises. Kiran giggled as she splattered some butter onto an aloo paratha. These old men met in the park less for the exercise and more for their daily dose of gup-shup—politics, cricket, some Bollywood starlet's cover photo on *Stardust*—and created a racket that rivalled the squawking of birds in the branches overhead.

The morning was colder than usual, and the tell-tale scent of saptaparna flowers announced that winter had arrived early and was setting in rapidly. Kiran noticed that the chill had sobered the delirious ecosystem around the mulberry tree. The branches, bereft of clusters of red-black fruit, carried only the weight of leaves half-eaten by silkworms. The ruckus of parakeets, crows and the invisible koel had given way to the hushed predatory sounds of cheels and vultures. She wondered if the news of the riot had stilled the banter of the group under the tree. Probably not. Major Budhwar was most likely discussing the tomato tendrils and baby mangoes that grew in his prize-winning vegetable garden. Or, he was raging about Jaspreet Singh's granddaughter Amrit, who routinely climbed the wall between the two houses and jumped into his cabbage patch. Ranbir Chawla was, she imagined, nodding off in the sunshine on a park bench.

Kiran had heard that Amrit had recently stomped out a row of poppies and beheaded young sunflowers in Major Budhwar's fabled nursery. She peeped out of the window to get a better view of the group. She couldn't spot Jaspreet Singh. Maybe he had stopped coming to the park. He was sensible to stay indoors these days; not like her Gursimran, who couldn't be convinced to stay away from the park until the riot subsided, or at least cut his hair. It would grow back; she knew it would grow back rapidly, in the fierce dark clusters that she loved to discipline with a variety of hair oils. But Gursimran was intolerant to even the mildest suggestion of a haircut. 'Don't you *dare* say that, *ever again*,' he had said to her, with a bite in his voice that had made her sob.

Kiran saw Ram Narayan Khanna talking animatedly to his gaggle of silver-haired friends. He was probably discussing the headlines in the morning paper. If anything were to happen to them, if Lala Kanshi Chand, maddened by fear and whispers of violence spreading to these parts of South Delhi, threw them out of the barsati, she would turn to Ram Narayan Khanna. She would fall at his feet; she would beg him to protect her and her stubborn but supple-limbed young husband who had no misgivings about jogging around the park in his thin cotton vest when the city was strewn with the dead bodies of those like him.

Lala Kanshi Chand, she knew, was not part of the group of septuagenarian exercisers. He had only recently moved into the neighbourhood with two generations of children and grandchildren that he had spawned with Kanta. The two-storey house, with this barsati, was protected from the inquisitiveness of neighbours by magenta lashings of bougainvillea. The general air of reticence around the Chand family had bred rumours about 'black money' and 'connections with corrupt bureaucrats'.

The renting out of this ramshackle room, to them, young and newly married, was seen by the neighbours like a hesitant attempt to open the wrought-iron gates of his home for a whiff of local air. But unkind remarks were overheard at parties that she and Gursimran were sometimes invited to. 'His dry fruit business in Chawri Bazar is a bit slow these days and he is *fleecing* this young couple,' a well-informed neighbour had said, nursing a glass of smuggled Scotch in one hand and holding a tender lamb chop in another.

'He will use the rent to send his grandchildren abroad, for higher studies. He doesn't want them to sell walnuts and almonds like he does,' another opinionated elder had said.

'Or he will buy his wife a polki-diamond set with the money,' a woman draped in jacquard silk had suggested, her long fingers interlaced around a glass of Virgin Mary.

Kiran had wondered if Lala Kanshi Chand did have connections with bureaucrats, fattened with the bribes of businessmen like him. If the rumour-mongers of this neighbourhood were to be believed, she would perhaps have to coax Gursimran into leaving this barsati for another, maybe even smaller room in the house of someone respectable. But for now, this was their home, and this was the bougainvillea-dappled little terrace on which she would soon be eating breakfast with Gursimran, whose footsteps she could hear on the stairs.

II

'He's not a monster, jaanu, he'll let us stay as long as we pay the rent and keep the noise down.' Gursimran grinned through mouthfuls of aloo paratha.

'What if that wife of his poisons his ears? What if she convinces him that we are a danger to the family? It was in the news...' Kiran's voice trailed off.

Gursimran stopped chewing.

'Were you watching the news? Why, jaanu? You know it upsets you. Please jaanu, everything that is happening, is happening *very far away* from us,' he managed to say, his words acquiring the sharp edge of a kitchen knife.

'It is spreading, Gursi. Only yesterday, Kanta-ji was saying that the goondas know which houses have Sikhs in them... They have a voters' list or something, jaanu...' Kiran's eyes filled up as she spoke, but she fought back the tears.

'We are safe here. We have friends in this neighbourhood,' said Gursimran as he pushed his plate aside and started to get dressed. He was about to tie a navy-blue turban around his head, but Kiran stopped him by grabbing one end of the fabric.

'Where are you going...jaa...anu... Don't you know that Dilli is under cur...cur...curfew?' she asked, her words an alarmed jumble.

'Let me buy some sabzi for the next few days. Who knows what might happen tomorrow? At least we will be well-fed before we...no...before *I* die...' he replied, winding the turban around his head.

'Hai Rabba! Don't talk like that Gursi...bite your tongue... bite your tongue now! You are not going anywhere...' Kiran grabbed his wrists as she wailed.

'I'll be back by the time that halwa is ready,' he said, staring at a pan in the kitchen which simmered with dollops of ghee. A pile of freshly shredded carrots lay on the counter. Kiran was making a batch of carrot halwa to acknowledge the first sting of winter. She would send some downstairs to Kanta and make her peace with the prying old lady. And she would not waste water when she was doing the dishes or washing clothes, so that Lala Kanshi Chand could no longer complain about the falling water levels in his precious tanks.

'They will see you in that pagri, riding your scooter…and… they will…' She choked on her words.

Gursimran kissed her before she could say anything else, and galloped down the stairs. She rushed to the kitchen window and cried out, 'Gursi! Don't go, Gursi. Hai Rabba, what should I do, Gursi O Gur…'

But Gursi was already kick-starting his old scooter.

III

'Hurry up, you don't have much time.' Lala Kanshi Chand stood in the barsati, his substantial bulk leaving very little space for anyone else to move, let alone do things with speed and efficiency.

Kiran was stuffing a small red suitcase with a few clothes that she had pulled out of her cupboard. The task was keeping her from breaking down completely. She had known it would come to this. He was throwing them out. He was leaving them on the streets to die. She stifled a wail and put some underwear, hidden under a dupatta, into the suitcase. She didn't want the old man, with that filthy glint in his eyes, to catch a glimpse of her panties.

'You don't have to take *everything* jaanu,' snapped Gursimran. 'Let's leave, *now*.'

A sudden anger flushed her cheeks and dilated her eyes. How dare Gursi talk to her like that, like a *typical husband*, in front of that Lala? It was humiliating enough to be evicted without warning, and now Gursi was adding to her shame by bullying her, goading her, telling her what to take and what not to. Let him live on the streets in his jogging vest and knickers; she would need a few more clothes to cover her in her hour of disgrace. And the riot, how would they survive that? It was a miracle that Gursi had returned home with a jhola full of vegetables. There were rioters everywhere, turning the city into a cremation ground full of burning pyres…even those new policemen from the border security forces could do nothing…even her Sache Patshah was deaf to her prayers…

They were being thrown out, and all Gursimran could do was shout at her. He hadn't questioned the landlord once, hadn't discussed the terms of the lease or the tenancy agreement. He had quietly agreed to vacate the barsati, and live on the footpath in a city raging over the murder of the Prime Minister.

'Get into the car,' thundered Lala Kanshi Chand. 'Do your shringar later; I don't have time to waste,' he hollered as he descended the stairs of the barsati.

Car? Was the old Lala planning to drive them to their deaths in his vintage Pontiac? Kiran sat down by the open suitcase for a long cry, but Gursimran slammed it shut and hoisted it over his shoulder, before grabbing her by the arm and dragging her out of their beloved barsati.

IV

The barsati was burned down that evening. Kiran heard the commotion of fire brigades and police sirens through a tiny window in the room in which she huddled with Gursimran.

Lala Kanshi Chand had driven them here, to Ram Narayan Khanna's house. They were to live in this little room till the riot subsided and the city was calmer. She had known all along that the rioters could identify the homes of Sikhs in the neighbourhood, and Lala Kanshi Chand's house, with its gigantic gateposts and iron fencing, was as vulnerable as the rows of matchbox-sized homes that had been set on fire in Trilokpuri.

This new room she found herself in was a storeroom for winter clothes and odd pieces of furniture, but at least it was built inside the house. It felt like a safe little pocket stitched to the high ceiling of the house. Kiran snuggled close to Gursimran on the narrow mattress. Blankets were stacked in the room from floor to ceiling. They pushed some of these into a corner to make room for their mattress. Kiran was not shuddering any longer, and after a long night fraught with unknown perils, she finally allowed herself to feel safe.

There was a soft knock on the door that made her sit up, vigilant for trouble. Gursimran grazed her fingertips with his lips before scuttling on his knees to open the door. The ceiling of the room hung close to the floor, and there wasn't enough space for the two of them to stand up straight.

Ram Narayan Khanna stood outside with two steaming mugs of milk.

'Three or four fire brigades are parked outside the Lala's house,' she heard Ram Narayan Khanna tell Gursimran.

'Wahe Guru! The family…is the family…was the family inside the house when it happened?' Gursimran asked in an unsteady voice.

'I don't know puttar, I can only pray that they are safe,' Ram Narayan Khanna replied hoarsely.

Kiran wept in the darkened storeroom, and muttered a quick, angry prayer to her Sache Patshah, who was supposed to protect his children but who was silent and ineffectual in the trouble that had fallen upon this city. She would go back to meet the old Lala. She would touch his feet for not abandoning them. She would pray, every day, for his business of almonds and walnuts and pistachios to expand beyond Chandni Chowk, beyond the capital, across continents.

Gursimran crept in with the mugs of milk. He offered one to her and said, 'Try and sleep, jaanu. It has been a long day…'

Sleep. What if someone poured kerosene on them as they slept? She held Gursimran close as she sipped the milk.

V

Kiran stood amidst the rubble of the barsati. How quickly a fortnight or so had gone by, she thought now, as she examined the remains of what was once her kitchen. Everything had been reduced to ashes—the wooden cabinet with its rows of ground spices and pickles in glass jars, the marble counter on which she chopped vegetables, the cups and plates, the three-legged chair. The rioters had thrown mashaals over the bougainvillea trees and the little garret had burned easily. The plants around the barsati—tulsi, jasmine, rose—had probably stoked the flames. Kanta, whom she met before climbing up the charred staircase to the barsati, informed her that the upper storey of the house had also caught fire, before the fire brigade had arrived.

She wondered where Lala Kanshi Chand was. It was still quite early in the morning, and this was the first time she had stepped out of Ram Narayan Khanna's house. The curfew had finally been lifted. Gursimran had left for work; he would probably resume jogging around the park in a day or two. He had been cranky during their confinement—he had tried to do a few push-ups, but had hit his head against the roof of the storeroom. Kiran hoped he would go back to the park soon—the bracing winter air and vigorous workout would make him less snappy.

She could see the group of men standing under the mulberry tree, from the terrace of the barsati, where the kitchen wall with its small window had once been. Major Budhwar was frowning as he spoke to Ranbir Chawla, who looked half-asleep, as usual. Jaspreet Singh was there—she had heard that a group of men had broken into his house too, but he had been saved. Someone had found a place for him to hide, was it Amrit, she wondered. But Amrit was too young to know what was going on.

She spotted Ram Narayan Khanna deep in conversation with someone. They stood a little apart from the group. From the massive frame and the manner in which he stood, with his arms akimbo, as though about to admonish someone, she could tell that the latest member of the septuagenarian group of exercisers was none other than Lala Kanshi Chand. Kiran smiled, for the first time after the riot.

Balbir & Sons

I

The cabinet smelt of naphthalene balls and old teakwood. Balbir Singh, slumped on a pile of pashmina shawls, felt his nose tingle. His face contorted in an effort to hold back the sneeze that was threatening to erupt and spray the new merchandise. The sneeze would also give him away. But at that moment, he was more worried about his stockpile of brocade silk, georgette, and embroidered Pashmina than he was about his safety.

Balbir had been crouching inside the wooden cabinet for only a few seconds. He had been pushed in by Kabir, his assistant at Balbir & Sons. Balbir's sons, disinterested in the family business of 'Bright Clothes for Bright Families'—a catchphrase he had coined and painted on the signage that clung to the front façade of the store—had moved a few years ago to join the suited-booted legions of the wealthier parts of the world.

'Kabir is all I have to assist with this store, with this life,' he would tell his cousin Jaspreet Singh, sighing into his cup of tea whenever they met. Balbir, who lived in Punjabi Bagh, had recently renovated his clothes' shop to look like a cheap replica of 'Debenhams-Shebanhams' and other departmental stores whose counters, shelves and lighting fixtures he had sketched on a trip to London to meet his younger son. As a result of his faithful ball-point recordings, the store was remodelled to become 'the only modern landmark in Punjabi Bagh', as he liked to brag to neighbours, customers and the occasional, befuddled foreign tourist seeking authentic pashmina in a city choking with fakes. The signage on the front of the shop, a tin rectangle that was the only element of the shop's architecture and ancillary features that gave away the store's and its owner's Punjabi Bagh antecedents, had the words '& Sons' on it as carefully painted ciphers of optimism. Balbir lived in the undiminished hope that his sons would some day return to the land of their birth and take over the family business. Until then, there was Kabir to help with the everyday hassles of running the shop—telling apart the big spenders from the mere admirers of the fabric on display; convincing the ladies of Punjabi Bagh that the hand-woven jamdanis and pure silks were very flattering to their thick waistlines and mountainous chests; getting wealthy and disinterested husbands to spend on their wives by deploying stealthy salesmanship: 'Just look at her, sir-ji, she looks like the bride you once brought home. Milk-and-honey in that peach zari sari. She will be honey sweet at home too if you get her the sari, sir-ji.'

Balbir visited Jaspreet often, seeking friendly banter and tea. Jaspreet lived in a neighbourhood in South Delhi where the roads were punctuated with parks and the sky was livid with congregations of sparrows, crows, and somersaulting parakeets bursting with song. Balbir enjoyed meeting Jaspreet's silver-haired neighbours, who had been sprawling under a mulberry tree in a local park every day for over twenty years, when they ought to have been exercising their arthritic joints. Conversation was always animated, and often marred with squabbles as the old men discussed this and that. They spoke of government dogmas that curtailed the lucrative schemes of new capitalists and drove the children to far-away countries. The recent antics of a cosmonaut who performed yoga as he floated in space made them try out creaky versions of sarvangasana and dhanurasana, which left them in tangled heaps on the grass. There was other news worthy of collective scrutiny—the predicament of a lawyer in the Kerala High Court who modelled for a Gold Flake cigarette advertisement and was subsequently suspended, led to an outbreak of cackling. 'If he can model at 59, then I can model at 62,' one of them had declared.

Balbir, a silent and baffled listener at first, had been coaxed into participating by the chatty old men. And he had joined in, adding with a casual assertiveness he did not feel, to the flawed logic and convoluted sentences of these neighbours. He wanted to impress these South Delhi businessmen and retired servicemen. He didn't want to embarrass Jaspreet by sitting under the tree only to pour himself cup after cup of spiced tea from a thermos that was always present and was handed around frequently as the men talked. His silence, or even his rambling in rounded syllables would be certain evidence of his Punjabi Baghness, and he couldn't risk being perceived as someone unexposed to posh South Delhi, its carpeted living rooms and cut-glass accents.

Over here in Punjabi Bagh, everyone called him Chacha. But his neighbourhood was different from South Delhi, although Hindu and Sikh refugees had settled in both areas after Partition. He was acutely aware, whenever he visited Jaspreet's home, that *his* Punjabi Bagh still bore traces of an intimacy typical of a refugee colony. Neighbours, who had once lived in tiny quarters and swapped recipes over cracked walls or borrowed a glass of milk for an unexpected visitor, still addressed one another in terms usually reserved for extended family. The camaraderie of the place had turned even complete strangers into distant relatives of some sort—elderly women were called Kaki, young boys, Kaka, and older men like Balbir were universally referred to as Chacha.

Jaspreet's park-going set, despite its thigh-slapping banter, was a conclave that did not trespass the boundaries of sophistication and good manners. So Major Budhwar, Jaspreet's neighbour, was called Major Saab, Ram Narayan Khanna, who was always the first to prompt an argument over the morning news, was called Khanna-ji, and Jaspreet was Mr Singh. No chachas or mamas or bhaisahibs or even uncles in that neighbourhood with its trimmed rose bushes and neat rows of Ashoka trees. Friendship, like the wrought-iron gates of their houses, opened up slowly and widely enough to allow familiarity to creep in, but not cloying affection.

Balbir tried to move inside the cabinet, but his turbaned head hit against the low wooden roof with a dull thud. He would have to be absolutely still, he scolded himself, or they would make a bonfire of his bones. A bonfire of human flesh, Pashmina, silk and teak wood. Already, he could smell something burning. He wedged an eyeball in the slim gap between the doors of the cabinet and tried to see what was going on in his store.

The sound of shattering glass reached Balbir and he knew that the rioters had broken the display window. He could hear a crowd of men chanting, 'Sardar ka bachcha, murdabad.' The smell of burning grew stronger—plastic and wool.

The curfew had just been lifted, and Balbir had raised the shutters of Balbir & Sons. That morning, he had dressed a family of mannequins inside the display window. A male mannequin stood next to a female mannequin. A child mannequin stood between them, its arms raised in a gesture of jubilation. With Kabir's help he had put onto their plastic bodies woollen garments that were part of the store's newest winter collection—fluffy pullovers, mufflers and pom-pom caps. Balbir had been pleased with the impact the mannequins had on the few passers-by who had ventured out. They glanced sideways as they walked, caught a glimpse of the scene inside the window, and smiled instantly, as though forgetting that they were walking down a street where the wail of police sirens was always close. Cotton-wool snowflakes were pasted on the window, to simulate winter in a city that had never known snowfall. The cheeks of the mannequin family, painted a deep crimson, and their large, almond-shaped eyes, with a spot of white inside the irises to heighten their gleaming merriment, suggested a snugness that was possible to achieve only within the confines of the shop window.

He wondered now if the rioters had torched the family of mannequins.

He had spoken to Jaspreet about a week earlier, on the day the Prime Minister had been shot dead. Jaspreet had whispered into the telephone receiver, as though merely mentioning the word 'riot' would bring a mob to his gate. Balbir should shut the store down for a few days and stay home, Jaspreet had advised, his voice weak.

And now he lay inside the storage cabinet, his long legs folded and pressing against his chest, feeling his heart hammer against his knees.

II

A splinter of light flickered through the gap between the cabinet doors, and Balbir caught a whiff of smoke. They had set the store on fire, he was certain. There was not much he could see through the slit; the images that formed outside were blurred and confounding. The rhythmic sound of 'Sardar ka bachcha, murdabad,' seemed to have moved closer—its muffled reverberations agitated Balbir. He restrained himself from bursting through the cabinet doors and shooting the rioters down with the pistol that lay inside a drawer near the cash counter.

The pistol was not his; he had intended to return it to its owner, but the curfew of the last few days had made it impossible to drive from one part of the city to another. It belonged to old Major Budhwar, whose vegetable garden was a botanical wonder. He had brought it to the park one evening in early October, when the mulberry tree, which had pelted them with long, wormy clusters of fruit in the summer, was a quiet canopy of perforated green. Balbir was visiting Jaspreet. Together, they had arrived at the park with jute mats to spread on the grass and a tiffin box full of mint-chutney sandwiches. Someone else—was it Ram Narayan Khanna, or that sleepy fellow, Ranbir Chawla?—brought tea in a plastic thermos. They were settling into their high-tea picnic when Major Budhwar, startled by a sparrow's droppings that had plonked onto his head from the branches above, had taken the pistol out from a pocket in his cotton half-pants, and had pointed it at the 'bird with diarrhoea'.

'Sit down, Major Saab, there's no need to use that. It's just a little bird.' Jaspreet had said, in the same tone he used to broker peace whenever his granddaughter Amrit erupted in snot and tears.

Balbir remembered how he had nearly choked on his sandwich when he saw the Major holding the pistol. The others had munched on their snacks and drained their plastic cups, unperturbed. They knew the Major had a weapon, and had probably seen him use it before to frighten every winged creature that had dared to swoop down for a mid-flight nibble of his beloved guava and mango trees.

'I'm not going to kill it...I'll just fire blank shots in the sky and empty the air space above us,' the old Major had clarified.

'Oye ji Major Saab, do you always carry that pistol to the park?' Balbir recalled asking him, smiling to himself now in the suffocating darkness of the cabinet.

'He carries it when he suspects that crows are flying too close to his pomegranate branches, that bees are making honey inside his red-rose petals, that pigeons are making love in his tomato and pumpkin alcove,' Jaspreet had twirled his luxuriant moustache and jibed.

'Monkeys...There were monkeys in my garden today, baring their teeth at me, scratching their stinking bottoms in front of *my* Sweetie and *your* Amrit, munching away on my guavas...I had to scare them away...' Major Budhwar had hissed at Jaspreet, taking aim, first at his friend and then at the mulberry tree under which they sat. 'Just think...just think Mr Singh, what if one jumps on your head right now, from that tree, and starts picking on your turban... How would you like that, haan? The pistol is for our safety, okay? Laugh...laugh all you want.'

The men had guffawed, falling about on the jute mat, spilling lukewarm tea on the quivering mounds of their bellies.

'Monkeys are such a menace everywhere. Even in Punjabi

Bagh they jump from the neem trees into people's terraces, making clotheslines collapse, running off with washed underwear...' Balbir had rambled, in an attempt to add to the mirth.

'Keep the pistol...Punjabi Bagh monkeys sound as bad as our South Dilli ones. You have a new shop Balbir ji, what if one red-arsed fellow gets in? Keep the pistol, I say...use it to keep them off your property,' Major Budhwar had bellowed, handing the weapon to Balbir.

Balbir had brought home the pistol, fearing that the old Major might pull the trigger on him if he refused. He never expected the simian crisis to become severe enough for him to use it. He had thought he would give it back to Major Saab soon.

But the riot had left the city numb. The pistol had remained with Balbir. And now, hiding inside the teak wood cabinet, he wondered if Kabir knew that it was in the shop.

III

'Sardar ka bachcha, murdabad.' The sound was close enough to make a nerve throb on Balbir's forehead, like a siren portending doom. He could hear fabric being pulled out and torn apart. A sudden stench made his nostrils twitch. If he sneezed, they would break the cabinet door immediately. Even if he didn't, they would find him cowering over a stack of embroidered Pashmina. Of what good was that windfall of a few seconds of life? He should jump out of the cabinet now and die like a sardar, like the son of a sardar, and not like a mouse caught in a trap.

He heard the shots—one, two, was there a third? —before he pushed open the cabinet doors and rolled onto the floor of his shop. He stood up and sneezed. The shop was empty but hazy; swirls of smoke stung his eyes and made them water. Rolls of silk, satin, georgette and crepe burned in steady pyres. Splintered glass carpeted the floor, the counters, and the broken drawers.

Balbir walked towards the front door of his shop, the shattered glass crunching underneath his feet. The mannequins lay burning in a heap of plastic limbs and nylon hair. Their synthetic skin melted together, turning all three—father, mother, and child—into one dismembered family bundle. A crowd hovered outside the front door. Balbir stumbled towards it. Where was Kabir? Had he run off after shoving Balbir into the cabinet? Had he left the store to be looted by these mad men?

The signage 'Balbir & Sons' dangled at a slant from the wall. Balbir noticed that stones had been hurled at the hand-painted board. It was dented, and was close to crashing down on the group below. The crowd seemed to disintegrate as Balbir approached it. He wondered why he wasn't already dead—there were so many rioters here, shouldn't one of them have, by now, thrown a tyre around his neck and set it alight? But the collective gaze of the murderers was transfixed upon a spot on the pavement. A man lay splattered in blood, his face crushed against the gravel. His white kurta-pyjama, slowly turning red, was similar to the ones worn by the men who surrounded his body.

Kabir stood closest to the body, his feet in a small puddle of blood. The pistol dangled from his hands, its metallic body glinting in the twilight.

'Kabir...Hai Rabba...Kabir...' Balbir managed to gasp. Even in his shock he wondered why the Major had handed him a loaded pistol to keep.

The yowling of a police siren seemed to rouse the rioters. Slowly, they began to walk away from the corpse of their dead companion. They marched on, chanting, 'Sardar ka bachcha, murdabad.'

Balbir stood in the premature dusk, staring at Kabir.

Just then, the police arrived. A canvas-top jeep nearly skidded on the road before jerking to a halt. An officer jumped out and walked towards Balbir, and Kabir, who stood somewhat unsteady near the fallen rioter. The officer looked baffled. And then, he saw the pistol dangling from Kabir's fingers. Quickly and wordlessly, he handcuffed Kabir and led him to the jeep. He lifted the canvas flap of the vehicle, and pushed Kabir in. The jeep coughed up dust before rattling off, its siren blinking red and blaring needlessly.

Balbir started to run after the jeep. 'Stop stop!' he panted, chasing the screeching vehicle. Arrest those madarchods...not him...not my Kabir! He has done nothing wrong...Stop... Please stop...'

The jeep turned into a wobbly speck. Balbir collapsed on the road, howling at a few early stars in the darkening sky.

Rioter

I

Hari washed his hands carefully at the tiny washbasin in the courtyard. He wanted to get rid of the day's grime before he ate lunch. He looked around and noticed that everyone else was already sitting cross-legged on the floor, bent over thalis of dal and rice, running their fingers through the liquefied mess to scoop out small mounds of food, which they hurriedly put into their mouths. Filthy fingers, which no amount of soap could clean, thought Hari as he scrubbed his hands under the brownish trickle of water. He was not particular about hygiene—he lived in a basti where the communal taps usually ran dry and an out-of-season cloudburst provided him the only opportunity for a bath that could wash away the congealed sweat of a prolonged summer. But he was glad that the blood that was drying into a crusty membrane, like a second skin on his palms, disintegrated the moment he scrubbed it with the half-melted piece of soap.

This lunch was his first substantial meal after months of scavenging for food in the city's garbage bins, overflowing with the greasy refuse of the well-fed. He was hungry—he was always hungry—but the sight of the thali with its gentle dunes of rice soaked in dal, and its piles of deep-fried vegetables on the side, stoked his appetite with an urgency that made him rush through his ablutions. There was no biryani, as far as he could see, no mutton curry, no fried parts of either bird or animal. Of what use are sleepy rioters, he thought. The meal was meant to nourish them for the work that lay ahead; it was not meant to swell their tummies with rich gravy. He would have to wash up quickly—what if the food ran out? He had killed for this meal, and he was prepared to die, but only on a full stomach.

The curfew had just been lifted, and this was a good day to kill all the Sikhs who had dared to open their shops, their karkhanas, their hotels and dhabas. He wondered how many areas they were expected to cover after lunch, as he rolled up his sleeves in anticipation of the meal and squatted on the floor with the other men. He was served lunch, finally, by party-workers who shovelled rice out of a brass pot and dropped it into his thali. He ate the food with a barbarity he had reserved for later, when he would pay for this meal by dragging a Sikh, or the son of a Sikh out of his house and set his hair on fire. Or burn the tyres of a bus as a warning to those who ventured out on the street. But for now, he was just a labourer, a contract-worker who had toiled through the day to earn this meal.

The soft mouthfuls of rice and dal reminded him of the meals his mother had once cooked. He remembered sitting on the floor of their mud hut with his brothers, sifting the rice on his thali with fingers caked with the filth of an afternoon spent burrowing through wheat fields, demolishing anthills, building mountains and valleys with the dark soil of his village. His hands were cleaner then, even though they were unwashed, he thought, as he licked a morsel off his fingers. He wondered if his mother would be horrified at the sight of him, sitting on the floor of a stranger's home, eating with a group of people he barely knew, but with whom he shared a common guilt.

Hari noticed that they were seated in neat rows similar to the ones that are formed at a langar. The prosperous and the poor, the fortunate and the wretched, the virtuous and the wicked—everyone sat and ate together at a langar. He had eaten at many, especially on days when he had spent his daily wage on a pack of beedis and a bottle of tharra. He recalled now, as he slurped the watery dal on his thali, the gurdwara's rich fare—a thick dal that was a mix of black gram and chickpeas cooked in pure desi ghee, spiced with cinnamon and cloves.

A sudden shame came over him and he felt his appetite vanish. Those langars had nourished him on days when the tharra burned his empty stomach. The meals, lovingly cooked by devoted Sikhs who recited favourite passages from the Guru Granth Sahib, or sang in praise of their Guru as they cooked their aromatic curries, would lull him into a pleasant slumber after a day spent carrying bricks or shovelling gravel. He had cut the very arms that had stirred simmering cauldrons of gravy and had fed him. He had slit the very throats that had recited the Japji Sahib or the Kirtan Sohila and had eased the fretful throb in his head, as he sat eating in a crowd of hungry believers.

He quelled the guilt with another mouthful and forced himself to focus on one of the party-workers who had stood up to address the group of men. They were to finish lunch as quickly as possible and move towards the centre of the city. They were to bring buses to a halt, and look for Sikh men crouching under the seats. If the conductor or any of the passengers tried to protect Sikh co-travellers, they were to burn the bus down.

When they reached Connaught Place, they were to break into all the garment, leather, and hardware stores owned by Sikhs. They were to deface that translucent pearl that lay in the heart of Connaught Place—Capital Residency, a glittering new hotel that was owned and run by an enterprising Sikh. They were to erase him. They would be paid at the end of the day for their work. Hari wanted to know if there was a rate the party-workers had arrived at—a few hundred rupees, at least, for every murder. But the amount was left unsaid; Hari's fingers worked furiously at mixing the dal and rice in his thali.

He chewed slowly as he evaluated the murders he had committed before lunch. He, and a few co-rioters had killed a young bridegroom, whose long hair, oiled by the loving fingers of a crowd of aunts, had caught fire easily. The bridegroom was sitting bare-chested and cross-legged in the verandah of his home, the soles of his feet dyed with henna, his hair coiled into a tight bun, waiting to be bathed in milk and turmeric before the wedding ceremony, when Hari had broken in with the rest of his gang. He had paused only for a few seconds to take in the loveliness of the tiny flat – the courtyard fence festooned with a few auspicious yellow and orange marigold strings – markers of subdued festivity in a city alight with funeral pyres. A turbaned uncle beat a dholak, loudly enough for a group of women to dance to its wayward rhythm, but not with the usual boisterous persistence that would have stirred and entire neighbourhood into joining in. The lifting of the curfew had obviously calmed this family; it had chosen not to postpone the wedding of a beloved son. Here they were, chachas and chachis, mausas and mausis, their hands on their thick waistlines, their bodies shaking to Punjabi songs that ended with a happy 'Hai Shava!' Here they were—demented relatives and a few neighbours—deaf to the cries of the dying, to the wails of the bereaved, as though the rioting of the last few days was already a distant memory. He would destroy the fragile beauty of the flat with oil and burning tyres, until even the embers had died.

He had wrestled the bridegroom to the ground. His gang members had pinned the boy's thrashing arms and legs to the verandah's uneven concrete. They had torched his hair with a matchstick. They had poured kerosene over his body, already slick with oil and a paste of chandan. Hari remembered how a heaving mass of bodies, draped in silk and clammy with the exertion of too much dancing had tried to wrench the rioters away from the bridegroom. But the young boy had burned readily, like an incense stick exuding chandan before shrivelling up.

Hari had also plunged a dagger into the bridegroom's chest before a wailing aunt could throw herself on the writhing body. The body was stilled but the wailing only grew louder as Hari and the other rioters left the house to find someone else to slaughter. The neighbourhood was predominantly Sikh and it was easy for him to find men he could butcher—they had been instructed to spare the women—but he had managed to murder only one other person. A septuagenarian who lay on a charpoy in the sunlit balcony of his home, who couldn't get up and run when Hari jumped across a wall and hoisted himself onto the balcony. The old man dropped his cup of tea—it stained his kurta before the blood did when Hari slit his throat with a dagger. He managed to gasp a final 'Wahe Guru' before dying.

The crashing of the teacup brought an elderly woman to the balcony. When she saw her husband with his throat slit, she howled in a brief spasm of grief, her body swaying from side to side, before running down a narrow flight of stairs with a teenage boy.

'A grandson,' Hari muttered, walking through the house, searching for other Sikh relatives lurking in cupboards and wooden cabinets. But he didn't chase the two of them—he knew they would not get very far; someone else from the gang would grab the boy and burn him alive on the street.

Two easy murders, Hari thought, as he continued to eat.

He would be paid a few hundred rupees only, unless he could kill more Sikhs after lunch.

The food was making him drowsy, and he longed for a nap. Maybe—the scavenger in him thought—he would not have to kill anyone now. There would be enough bodies strewn on the streets anyway; he could simply search the mass of putrid flesh for broken arms or legs or even whole heads that had been hacked. He could put the severed body parts in a sack and show them to the party-workers, demanding at least three or four thousand rupees for the thoroughness of the murders. Were body parts enough proof that whole Sikh men had been butchered? The party workers had not bothered to tell them.

He didn't really want to kill any more.

Hari wondered if they would be offered a cup of tea in the evening, after they had ripped open Connaught Place and picked at its entrails. He looked forward to his next break. But, before that, there was work to be done. And money to be earned—enough money to buy tharra every day and have it with deep-fried pakodas.

II

The crystal chandelier hanging from the ceiling of the Capital Residency, with its antique cutwork filigree, refracted the light in the dining hall in ways that made Ramanjit Singh say out loud, often to himself, 'What a sight, a rainbow inside!' He would watch with delight as beams of light bounced off the polished silverware, or caught the glimmer of a diamond nose-pin that clung to the delicately flared nostril of a guest, or heightened the luminosity of a dark pair of eyes, or the flush of cheeks bulging with a mouthful of tandoori chicken.

Capital Residency was Ramanjit Singh's dream that had taken the shape of a domed, chandeliered, and cobalt velvet four-star hotel. He was determined to earn a fifth star by importing an espresso machine from Italy that would introduce this city to the joys of a frothy cappuccino, and turn his coffee shop into a 'multi-speciality restaurant'. He was an optimist; he believed that a little imagination and a 'lump-sum investment', which included lining the pockets of the capital's bureaucrats with surplus change, could help him accomplish everything he had set out to do.

The coffee shop had been almost empty for the last few days; that, he knew, was because of the bloody riot. He had instructed the staff to keep the gates of the hotel locked, even during the day, so that the goondas who were running loose in the city would think the hotel was closed for business. But he had not shut it down; how could he when there were still a few guests who had checked in just before the riot? Thick velvet curtains had been drawn over the windows, and the crystal chandelier had not been lit for a few days. But the guests were fed, and taken care of, with silent efficiency and utmost courtesy, even though most of the staff had not reported to work.

And now, with the bloody curfew relaxing, Dilli's kebab-and-chaap lovers would soon be back to his coffee shop...

but...where was the staff? Had everyone been killed in this bloody city?

As soon as the bloody looting and killing ended, he would import a chef from Italy along with the espresso machine, to make the dining experience a really 'intercontinental one'. Apart from the usual chicken and mutton dishes—Butter Chicken, Kadhai Chicken, Mutton Dopyaza, Rogan Josh—there was nothing on the menu to indicate the chef's multi-cuisine proficiencies. While the restaurant catered to local Punjabi taste, Ramanjit Singh was keen to include a few dishes like 'macaroni-cheese from Italy' to attract foreign tourists, the 'hippie-shippies with burnt skin and bleached hair', who roamed the corridors of Connaught Place's Inner Circle with gigantic rucksacks slung across their shoulders, studying travel guides as they walked, bumping into sellers of chana-chor-garam and occasionally, the cylindrical pillars that stood like sentinels on the roundabout passages.

He would hire a bloody foreign chef, he decided, as he walked towards the kitchen to find out why Table Two—the only table that was occupied in the coffee shop—hadn't been served. He would hire new staff—liveried waiters, housekeeping that actually changed the sheets after a guest vacated a room, and a smartly dressed lady at the reception who was not an aunt or an unmarried second cousin. He would redecorate and repair even though everything was still new, if that was what it took to get the foreigners to stay in his hotel.

Preoccupied with thoughts of an imminent sacking, he

pushed open the door to the kitchen and found the chef chopping a tomato in a silent rage. His underlings, who had been hired to cut vegetables and clean fowl and fish while he invented grand recipes and stirred pots, were nowhere to be seen. He was alone, working in a kitchen with naked birds spread-eagled on the counter, waiting to be marinated. A pumpkin had fallen to the floor and lay smashed in a puddle of pulp and juice, its seeds scattered in every direction.

'Arre Ravidas, why this bloody mess?' Ramanjit Singh asked, waving his hands.

'Arre sahib, what can a poor man like me do, all alone, cooking, cleaning, and even serving,' Ravidas replied, chopping the tomato with renewed intensity.

'Where is everyone? Are they asleep? Or dead?' thundered Ramanjit Singh. He picked up an onion that had rolled to the floor, and continued, 'Guests are waiting for their food, but this kitchen has closed down without my permission.'

'When *they* walk in and slit our throats, *they* will not take your permission, sahib,' said Ravidas. He lifted a chicken and tore its tender flesh with a kitchen knife—a melodramatic gesture that irritated his employer.

'Who will walk in? Nobody can walk in without my permission. What bloody nonsense you talk, Ravidas!' Ramanjit Singh raised his voice, but was careful not to shout at the chef.

'Sahib, curfew or no curfew, anything can happen at anytime...most of the staff is still at home...only I am here, sahib, only I am here...' said Ravidas, his steady voice threatening to break, as he finished chopping the tomato.

Ramanjit Singh grew silent. He had seen the news on TV. A beauteous newsreader insisted that the situation was under control, although he knew that Dilli was still tense. But his guests—a businessman from Meerut and an elderly couple who was scheduled to drive to Agra as soon as it was safe—were waiting for a meal. They would have to be served, and he would do it himself, if everyone else was at home, hiding under their mattresses like bloody chicken.

'Staff or no staff, we will continue to work, okay? You prepare the dishes, and *I* will carry them to the coffee shop,' Ramanjit Singh said, as he fumbled in the kitchen cabinet for a bottle opener. He found it in a dark corner, amidst a mess of broken china and soiled napkins, and used it to open a bottle of Campa Cola. The bottle fizzed as the crown yielded to the pressure of the opener. He poured the bubbly liquid into a glass and placed it on a tray. He balanced the tray on the palm of his hand and left the kitchen, turning around one last time to say to his chef, 'As long as I am alive, I will serve, okay?'

He walked down the long corridor from the kitchen to the coffee shop, holding the tray of Campa Cola slightly above his shoulder. The stained-glass mirrors that lined the walls multiplied his reflection, and he was pleased at the sight of several Ramanjit Singhs walking alongside him.

When a reflection disintegrated and shards of glass fell on the corridor, he realized that someone had thrown a stone at a mirror. When the walls reflected strange faces—their eyes glinting like splintered glass, their mouths covered with white cloth—he knew with a sudden dread that those bloody goondas had broken into his hotel. He felt a pair of coarse hands grab him, as the tray tumbled to the floor, soaking him in Campa Cola. He tried to wrestle with the hands, but felt himself pushed towards the floor by muscular arms.

He smelt the kerosene before his skin began to scald.

His burning body, with its flailing arms and wild locks, thrashed about on the polished marble corridor before one of the men stilled it by pouring more fuel on his torso and stoking the live bundle of bones, flesh, and hair.

III

After they murdered Ramanjit Singh, the rioters walked into the coffee shop to find only a few guests, trembling as they huddled together, awaiting their death. The businessman from Meerut had opened a window and was trying to jump out of it, as one of the rioters approached him with a can of fuel. He was caught and his throat was slit—butchered on the dining table, despite his short hair and clean-shaven face.

The elderly couple was spared—the wife had been chanting the Gayatri Mantra and had fallen to her knees when one of the rioters placed a bloodied knife on her husband's heaving chest.

'We are not from here, Hai Ram, Hai Krishna, Hai Bhole Nath let us go,' she wailed.

'Hai Ram,' she cried out again. 'Have mercy on us!' She

nearly fainted at the feet of one of the ruffians. But the knife was slowly removed, before it could puncture her husband's soft flesh, and she was made to stand next to him. Trembling, she joined her hands in gratitude as the rioters withdrew.

The rioters walked into every room of the small hotel, setting the upholstery on fire, breaking porcelain tea cups and bone china dinner plates, plunging their daggers and knives into thick mattresses to check for guests lying between the covers. They found no one in the rooms.

Before the rioters left the premises, they helped themselves to mattresses and blankets, to fluffy towels and bed linen, to stainless steel bathroom fittings that could be sold for a good price, to bars of Lux soap and unused tubes of toothpaste that could also be sold. They unplugged the gigantic black telephone that stood at the reception desk and carried it with them. And as a parting gesture of annihilation, they unhinged the crystal chandelier from its hook on the vaulted ceiling of the coffee shop. It swayed as its tear-drop baubles refracted the yellow light of the room into broken rainbows, before it came crashing down. It lay on a heap in the middle of the coffee shop, a cut-glass leviathan, splendid even in ruin.

IV

Hari did not participate in the burning of Ramanjit Singh. And he was not with his gang when they plundered Capital Residency. He was in the kitchen. A whiff of grilled meat had distracted him as he had walked up the stairs of the hotel, and he had broken away from the rioters to follow the aroma.

The kitchen, with its piles of chopped vegetables and pots of simmering kormas, roused the scavenger in Hari. He burrowed deep into the burning embers of a tandoor, scalding his arms as he pulled out a chicken roasting inside, seasoned with curd, black pepper, and ginger. He dipped a freshly baked naan into a pot of tender lamb curry. He lapped up a vessel full of creamy kheer, licking the sides to get every morsel of it.

He opened the kitchen cabinet, searching for other treats to feast on or to hoard—and pulled out the chef.

Startled, Hari reached for his dagger to stab the quivering man. But the scent of the food distracted him and he paused to ask the chef, 'Are you the khansama?'

Ravidas nodded vigorously.

'Did you make all this?' Hari continued, gripping the chef by the neck.

'Ji haan! I made everything today,' Ravidas managed to sputter. Tears rolled down his greasy face. He cursed himself silently for coming to work today, and not staying at home, like so many of the staff. Over the years, his dedication to cooking the finest curries in Delhi had caused him much grief—a strained marriage that had finally snapped because he worked long and erratic hours at Capital Residency; diabetes, for he tasted every dessert he prepared; premature grey streaks in his thick hair. But he had not anticipated losing his life for the sake of cooking a few dishes for waiting guests.

He knew that Ramanjit Singh had been killed, and that a similar fate awaited him. He had heard a commotion outside the kitchen, and had promptly hidden inside the odds-and-ends cabinet. The muffled sounds of wailing and Ramanjit Singh's final 'Wahe Guru' reached him through the closed door of the cabinet, and he sobbed softly in the darkness, knowing that he would never see his quick-tempered but large-hearted boss again.

'Don't kill me, I'm a Hindu,' he whimpered as Hari held him by the collar and pressed the dagger against his neck.

'Please,' he cried, 'my children will be orphaned. What have they done to deserve this?'

Hari considered the question. What had anybody done to deserve *this*? And what had he done to deserve his life—as a scavenger, as a contract worker with irregular wages, and now, as a hired killer who was not even sure why he was supposed to go after all the Sikhs in the city? He had seen grainy images of a body covered with marigold garlands, lying inside an open coffin, on the television set in the tharra shop. Was that the Prime Minister? Did her death have something to do with the sardars he sometimes drank with and lay on the footpath with, in a tharra stupor?

The news of the past few days was a muddle in his head. The only thing he knew for certain was his insatiable hunger. If only he could eat without having to kill, if only he could go back to the construction site he had been removed from—he would lift bricks in the scorching sun for the rest of his life, and not waste his money on tharra.

'Can you make gajar ka halwa?' he asked Ravidas, slackening his grip around the chef's neck.

Ravidas managed to smile. 'I can make the best gajar ka halwa in Delhi,' he said, relief coursing slowly through his veins.

'Then make it, now,' said Hari, as he let go of the chef.

With unsteady hands, Ravidas grated a few carrots for the halwa, silently thanking all the benevolent deities he had never prayed to until now, for his culinary skills and his ability to work under pressure.

V

After ransacking Capital Residency, the rioters reached Punjabi Bagh. It was early evening, and they headed towards a few large shops that had lifted their shutters and opened their doors as soon as the curfew was eased. They would pelt stones at display windows. They would climb over walls and throw a mashaal into the pruned rose bushes of the wealthy Sikh merchants who lived and worked there. They would loot their homes, their offices, their glittering showrooms.

Hari, who walked through the street like a sleepwalker, his senses dulled by the food he had consumed, wondered if anyone would notice if he just stood outside the premises they were moving towards and shouted 'Sardar ka bachcha, murdabad,' with some of the other men in the group. Slogan-shouting was a critical part of the rioters' campaign to rupture the tenuous calm of the city. Hari knew that killing sardar men was more lucrative than proclaiming on the streets that they deserved to die, and he decided to collect body parts the moment a Sikh was murdered, as he had planned earlier. He would then ask for his payment from the party-worker, and leave the city in a few days. He would find a permanent job in a small furniture factory on the outskirts. He would work with tools—hammers, screwdrivers, saws—and forget that he had ever held a lathi or a dagger in his hands.

The rioters surrounded Balbir & Sons, a garment store. Hari was fascinated by the family of mannequins that stood at the display window. They were wearing colourful winter clothes. Their dilated eyes and pink faces made Hari wish he could touch them—especially the child mannequin, whose shiny, plastic cheeks he wanted to pinch with his rough hands.

Someone shattered the glass of the display window. The family of mannequins was torched. Hari watched the painted eyes of the dolls melt, their smudged and leaky irises a silent plea to stop the mayhem.

'Gudda aur guddi aur unka bachcha, teeno seedha parlok!' he mumbled to himself, as he watched the flames consume the faces that smiled through the inferno.

A group of men broke into the showroom. They walked in through the shattered window and made a bonfire of the scarves, sweaters, and Pashmina shawls on the shelves of the store. Hari remained outside, with a band of sloganeers. He would go into the showroom when the proprietor was killed, to pick up the limbs.

'Sardar ka bachcha, murdabad,' they shouted into the winter evening.

'Sardar ka bachcha murdabad,' Hari repeated feebly, longing to get back to his basti.

'Khoon ka badla, khoon,' the group shouted.

'Khoon ka badla…' Hari managed to say, when a shot rang out. The crowd of rioters inside Balbir & Sons ran out. The sloganeers standing outside dispersed. But Hari collapsed on the pavement, as the bullet rent his chest. A few sparrows chirruped into the twilight, before the sloganeers resumed their chanting.

'Khoon ka badla, khoon,' they hollered, stumbling over Hari's body as they made their way down the street.

Vagabonds

I

A wooden platform, tiny wheels attached to its four sides, slithered between the rows of cars, buses and the occasional bullock cart as the lights turned red at the Bhikaji Cama intersection. Bhola, perched on top of the platform, navigated it expertly by pressing his bandaged hands against the road and pushing it forward. The wheels scratched the pockmarked surface of the road, and Bhola inched ahead, humming fragments of a song he had recently heard on the Murphy radio that stood on a shelf in Kallu's Chicken and Mutton Shop: 'Hum bande hain pyar ke, mange sabki khair.'

Bhola's legs were useless stumps that protruded out of his mobile platform. Whether they had been amputated in a hospital or smashed to pulp on some footpath was a mystery. But the myth of limbs that once functioned—tight calves, football thighs, hairy toes—was reinvented and refurbished with startling details by the younger urchins who shared the footpath with him. 'He could even chase the Rajdhani Express, but one day, he threw himself on the track and the train crushed his legs…just like, just like…sugarcane is crushed, for ras,' said thirteen-year-old Bittoo, who sold balloons and 'googlis'—eyewear with cellophane paper of magenta, parrot green and cobalt blue pasted on the plastic lenses—at the intersection. Satisfied with the impact the sugarcane simile had on his audience, Bittoo proceeded to explain why Bhola had decided to lie on the railway track one morning. 'Rekha,' he said, 'Rekha ditched Bhola… She ran off with an old seth. He was rich. Bhola was poor. And Rekha was a kutti who panted over money…'

Bhola knew that the footpath-dwellers gossiped about him in loud whispers. Despite his obvious handicap, he was the only one who made a decent living begging at the intersection. The coins that jangled in his tin bowl were enough to buy some mutton from Kallu's Chicken and Mutton Shop now and then. At other times he bought the cheaper offal, which he would cook in an old saucepan, the only utensil he possessed, in a corner of the pavement. He always shared his weekly mutton or gurday-kapooray curry with everyone else who lay sprawled on the footpath, or polished the leather shoes of the wealthy, or sold balloons, hand mirrors, plastic combs and eyewear at the crossing. On days like these, there was always enough cash to pay off the constable on duty, so he wouldn't interrupt the feasting ragamuffins by tapping the footpath with his lathi or by overturning the saucepan with its simmering gravy or by holding a beggar's offspring up in the air and threatening to throw the wailing child on the road to split open the skull, and to supply more meat for a spicy brain curry.

There was a raggedy sweetness about Bhola that made strangers who looked out of the windows of their Fiats and Ambassadors drop a coin or two in his bowl. The slight tilt of his head, the timbre of his voice—deep and yearning for love, or soft and lilting, free of the pain that life hurled at him every day—drew the attention of the giver of alms to his face, to his lips parted in a half-smile that contained all the melancholia of Bhikaji Cama on any day of the week, to the songs he mumbled as he raised his tin bowl to the level of a car window. The grotesque stumps that dangled uselessly from the platform were ignored, or they merely enhanced the urgency of his plea for a little spare change to buy a cup of tea and a piece of mathri to dip into it. Commuters were not repelled by him, like they were by the over-zealous Bittoo, who was not a beggar but a seller of plastic knick-knacks, and was not as prosperous as Bhola.

Begging was a subtle art, Bhola knew, and he was a natural at it. The wobbly platform, his outstretched arms and careful selection of songs, all of these lent his destitution the allure of an actor in the latest blockbuster, whose fate had faltered into filth and squalor, but who would soon emerge from the blows of destiny, win a lottery and live happily ever after in a palatial house with a buxom lover. He encouraged his companions on the footpath to invent stories about his crippled legs and bandaged hands; the myths enhanced his stature as a pitiable but noble creature. He stoked their imagination by offering incomplete sentences that lingered in the air, and dwindled off into deep sighs. 'I was sleeping on a charpoy, under the stars, when my father came into the courtyard and hit me on the legs with his stick...' he would say. Or, 'Polio... The doctors said "Polio!" My mother beat her chest...' Or, 'I was chopping an onion in a dhaba, to pay for my tea and mathri...there was a Kishore Kumar song on the radio...I didn't notice that I had chopped my fingers till the onion became red...' He noted that traffic was dense today; this made him sing a little louder. The curfew had just been lifted; schools had reopened in the city and Bhikaji Cama was clogged with cars and buses. The intersection looked busy, just the way he liked it. Bustling intersections were good for a day of lucrative begging. During the curfew, when not even a cyclist had ventured out, he had nearly starved. He had been reduced to scavenging for food in the city's garbage bins, like his rag-picker friends. It had been mortifying for a beggar of his stature to be seen foraging through refuse for a few crumbs. The murder of the Prime Minister had been bad for business; all he really wanted was for this city to forget about it, to get into its cars and press on the accelerator, to slow down at Bhikaji Cama intersection and roll down a window whenever he tapped on it with his tin bowl.

II

It was still early and the intersection was unusually crowded. Normally, the latter part of the day was rush hour, when buses crammed with commuters, cavalcades of white Ambassadors with red lights flashing on their roofs, matchbox-shaped Premier Padminis, and that new car, the Maruti 800, ignored the traffic signals and lurched ahead, to the only destination they had in common: home. In the mornings, traffic was sluggish, as though reluctant to make its way to work or school or Parliament. But today was different. Bhola sensed an impatience in the 7-a.m throng on the road. Roads sedated into an uneasy calm by the day and night curfew, which lasted for two weeks after the Prime Minister was shot, now buzzed with the haste of those passing through.

The public is happy to get out and move, thought Bhola, as he tapped on the window of a caramel-brown Premier Padmini. 'Hum bande hain pyar ke, mange sabki khair,' he sang softly, as the window of the passenger seat was rolled down. A gust of eau-de-cologne blew out of the car and enveloped Bhola in a tangerine-jasmine mist, which, for a few seconds, invited him into a world he did not belong to. A world of lace table cloths and long-stemmed roses in crystal vases. A world of hot baths, alarm clocks, and VCR dinners.

A woman with a short mop of dark curls peeped out of the window. Bhola appraised her with lowered but shifty eyes as she rummaged through her handbag for loose change. Patches of talcum powder were visible on her neck. Her slim gold bangles tinkled as her hand dived into a pocket inside her bag. 'Hum bande hain pyar ke...' he sang. But he could tell that she was already convinced that he was a person of love, who wanted her to be happy. He saw her hand emerge from the bag with a coin, a shiny twenty-five paisa. She adjusted the pallu of her betel-leaf green silk sari, which had shifted slightly from her bosom to reveal a hint of cleavage and a string of off-white pearls around her neck. She pulled at it and covered her chest completely before putting the coin in Bhola's tin bowl. She smiled as he saluted her with his bandaged hand, but caught a whiff of him and crinkled her nose.

'Best not to raise my arm, these memsahibs can smell my armpits even from their cars,' Bhola scolded himself, as the lights turned green and he made his way to the pavement. He would spend a few minutes at the tea stall off the road, under the shade of a devil tree. Maybe a kind babu, reading the *Navbharat Times* on a wooden bench outside the stall would offer him a cup of tea.

The stall was full of customers, sipping tea from small, conical glasses, in the November fog. Bhola positioned his platform near a counter, where a saucepan simmered with a milky-brown liquid. A lanky boy, who wore nothing but a thin cotton vest perforated with holes, and a pair of half-pants that shuddered and flapped in the skin-dimpling breeze, crushed a few cardamom pods and sprinkled them into the liquid. When the tea had formed an avalanche of bubbles in the pan, the boy removed it from the stove and poured it messily into glasses placed in rows on the counter. Before he carried the tea to waiting customers, he glanced meaningfully at Sadho Bhai, the owner of the stall, who sat behind a counter lined with glass jars full of mathri, namak pare, glucose biscuits, and orange, hard-boiled sweets.

Bhola observed the two—the portly employer and his fawning employee—reaching a silent agreement. Sadho Bhai nodded almost imperceptibly, but Bhola, who watched them closely, noticed the folds of Sadho Bhai's chin move up and down, twice. Almost immediately, the boy handed Bhola a glass of tea before walking past him to serve paying customers waiting in the cold. Bhola bowed deeply, his hands folded around the warm glass, to express his gratitude. Sadho Bhai's many chins moved up and down, yet again, to acknowledge the gesture. But when Bhola began to sing, 'Hum bande hain pyar ke...' Sadho Bhai rotated the large knob of the radio on the shelf with the jars of crumbly snacks. It hissed and whined before the voice of an announcer became audible. Bhola's song was drowned by All India Radio's distorted transmission. He pushed his platform ahead and positioned himself against the wooden leg of a table, around which sat a group of tea drinkers.

Conversation faded as the voice of the announcer rolled into the air like the fog, thick with news. After days of rioting, the capital city had grown calmer, the voice said, as the men sipped their tea. The police had brought the situation under control and law and order had been restored. Schools and colleges had reopened.

Bhola watched them snigger—the office-goers, the ex-servicemen in their canvas shoes, the slouchers whose tea turned cold before they put the glass to their lips, the frantic peddlers of rumour and scandal, who finished the spiced brew in one long gulp and raised their hands for a refill—when the announcer droned on about law and order. One of them, an elderly man who wore a maroon cardigan over a thin cotton kurta-pyjama, folded the newspaper that lay on his lap and flung it across the table.

'Police, haan,' he said to the group around the table. 'The entire police force is harami. It has let the sardars die on the streets like dogs.'

'Haan, haan…this radio-shadio news is cow dung…there is no laaah and no aarder in Dilli,' said another, slightly younger man, who dipped a glucose biscuit in his tea as he spoke.

'And…oh ji…listen to the latest stupidity…schools and colleges are opening. Now the riot-makers will pull out sardar children from school buses and burn them alive on the main road,' said a third middle-aged man who wore a monkey cap, which covered his head and neck. Only his eyes, nose and lips were visible through a gap in the woollen fabric.

'But the schools can't remain shut forever. I am so happy my grandchildren have gone back to school…all they did was listen to *Binaca Geetmala* on the radio…at full volume…I am deaf in one ear but even I knew that the radio was too loud…' said the elder in the maroon cardigan.

'I am not mourning for her…Mmm, actually I think it's good for our country that the Prime Minister is dead. So many people were killed inside the golden gurudwara, because she woke up one day and decided that terrorists were hiding there…' ventured the glucose-biscuit eater.

'Shhhh…don't say such things in public,' said the man who wore the monkey cap. He lowered his voice and continued,

'Even these mud walls have ears. You never know who is listening. What if someone comes from behind and pours a can of kerosene on you…'

'Then let me die for speaking the truth. You think I am scared? So many of my Sikh friends have died in the riot. Just the other day, a sardar taxi-driver I knew was killed for driving a pregnant woman to the hospital—when everyone else was hiding inside cupboards and under mattresses during the curfew,' the biscuit-eater bit into one with vehemence, and continued. 'She was already in labour; her husband only had a two-wheeler; the neighbours refused to help. Only this poor taxi driver agreed to drive them…he was caught and a tyre was thrown around his neck. The tyre was set on fire… God knows what happened to that howling woman and the baby…'

Bhola wondered whether he should move a little closer to the table. The conversation was of little interest to him; they could go on talking till dusk and beyond. All he really cared about was whether the group at the table would throw him a coin, or a biscuit. But just then, the lights at the intersection turned red. Bhola decided not to hover like a fly over the tea-drinkers, but to find a well-scrubbed family in a car, to charm with his song into parting with spare change.

III

A Bajaj scooter grazed the white lines of the zebra crossing, but stopped just in front of it when the lights turned red.

Bhola crouched at the entrance of the tea stall, waiting for the traffic to stop, so he could twist and turn his platform to get to the scooter. He used his instincts to single out the pair on the two-wheeler—a Sikh father and son. They waited at the crossing, their old scooter sputtering. Their turbans announced the lifting of the curfew. The son, a boy of seven or eight in school uniform, had his arms around his father's ample girth as he rode pillion.

'Look at that sardar, taking his son to school, look, look, they are not scared…of…of the…men…with lathis…of…the police…' Bhola said to no one in particular before hurtling towards the pavement. He would make his way to the pair on the scooter and bless their travels across this city with all the filmy songs he knew about good luck and divine protection. They would be so pleased with him that they would throw him a five-rupee—no, a ten-rupee—note!

The wheels on Bhola's platform squealed, resisting the gravel of the road, as he pushed ahead to reach the scooter before the signal changed. He was about to arrive at the zebra crossing when he noticed that the lights had, in fact, turned green, but the rows of cars and buses and mini-vans hadn't moved. The usual sounds of engines rasping to a start, car horns peep-peeping, and bicycle bells tring-tringing their way out of the Bhikaji Cama intersection were missing. The road was silent and watchful, the gentle whirr of engines like an erratic heartbeat, which, upon sensing menace, would stop at any moment.

Bhola could see the scooter he had been pushing his platform towards; a few men had formed a small circle around it. They hovered around the scooter, iron rods in hand, inching closer. The sardar on the scooter looked straight ahead, his knuckles white as his hands gripped the handlebars, his spine erect, as though not acknowledging the danger would avert it. His son clung to him, burying his face into his father's back. Bhola couldn't tell if the little boy was crying or not, but he knew that the men, who had brought the traffic at Bhikaji Cama crossing to a stupefied halt, were about to burn the father-son pair alive, on the road. He could see one of them unscrewing a tin can.

Was Bhola going to watch innocent sardars die on this intersection, *his* intersection, as he crouched on his platform like a useless cripple, a beggar who stank of the sewer? He would have to do something, quickly, and prove that he really was the kind of hero whose songs he sang to get commuters to fling coins into his bowl. The group of rioters had thrown the sardar on to the road. His son kept sitting on the scooter, his body shaking. One of the men was about to pour the kerosene when Bhola blew a whistle.

It was a pink, plastic whistle, the kind his balloon-salesman friend Bittoo sold at the intersection. Its shrill 'Pfree... rrrrreeee...pfreeeee' alarmed the crows and sparrows on the neem tree into silence, but stirred up the vagabonds of Bhikaji Cama. Out they came, swarming over the footpaths—the maimed, the pock-marked, the pus-infected, the one-eyed, the limbless. They hobbled across the street on crutches or lunged ahead on wooden platforms like Bhola's or crawled on their limbs.

The army of vagabonds reached the spot where the sardar lay, trembling and doused in kerosene. Swiftly, the derelicts parted the crowd that had circled the sardar. They rode their platforms through the limbs of the rioters, startling the men into dropping their iron rods. Sly urchins clung to the feet of the rioters; one of them started to wipe the shoes of the man who held the can of kerosene. He rubbed his rag expertly on the filthy shoes, singing the anthem of all shoeshine boys: 'Mera joota hai Japani!' The man dropped the canister in shock, and pushed the shoeshine boy away.

'Mera joota hai Japani,' sang the other urchins, clinging to the feet of the rioters, touching them with suppurating skin, breathing their putrid breath on startled faces. The rioters slowly moved away from the scooter.

'Chee chee, haramzada!' they shrieked, as the beggars touched them here, poked them there. 'Bhag, madarchod!' they yelped, trying to free their legs from the grip of the urchins.

Bhola hobbled through the mayhem created by his loyal friends from the pavements in and around Bhikaji Cama intersection, hollering the song about being a man of love. Bittoo joined the group of revellers too; he made bubbles from a soapy liquid in a small plastic container, and blew them at the rioters. The commotion lasted long enough for the sardar, who lay sprawled on the road, to get up, grab his son from the scooter, and run across the road.

When one of the rioters noticed the sardar and his son fleeing, he lurched forward, grabbing his iron rod as he tried to run after the Sikh. But Bhola grabbed his ankles and sang his song of love, and Bittoo blew a large bubble, which erupted on the rioter's face, covering it with foamy liquid. Enraged, he picked up the can of kerosene that lay forgotten on the road, and threatened to pour it on Bhola. When Bhola continued to croon, his delight increasing as the rioter fumed, he poured the fuel on the scooter's front tyre. The rioter then lit a match and threw it on the tyre. The rubber exploded in flames, dispersing the crowd of vagabonds and the rioters they clung to.

Bhola slurred, 'Hum bande hain pyar ke, mange sabki khair,' as he pushed his platform towards the pavement. The burning tyre put an end to the singing and dancing at the crossing. The rioters disappeared into a blanket of fog. Engines wheezed, traffic started to move.

'We are people of love,' hummed Bhola, 'We wish you well...'

IV

Bhola reached the tea stall, where he was greeted with a cascade of coins. Tea-drinkers, newspaper-readers and everyone else who had gathered to watch the sardar burn now surrounded him. He was the hero of Bhikaji Cama intersection. Someone threw a red rose into his bowl. Sadho Bhai emerged from behind the counter and offered him a glass full of tea, with extra milk and sugar.

Sala haramis, thought Bhola. They just sat here, sipped their tea, and watched as a sardar was nearly roasted, like chicken inside a tandoor. His people, his stinking lepers and urchins, had hearts made of pure gold biscuits—the type smuggled across continents in briefcases, in Hindi films. His filthy madarchods were better any day than this suited-booted crowd, which could sit on its gaand and discuss the Prime Minister's death and the murder of the city's Sikh men from morning till evening, but could do nothing to save a man's life.

A school bus slowed down at the intersection. Girls in maroon cardigans peeped out of open windows, staring at the fallen scooter, and the rings of flames that slowly consumed its metallic body. A few of the girls placed lace handkerchiefs on their delicate, upturned noses as the bus picked up speed and crossed the intersection.

Convent-school girls, they don't know anything except birthday parties and memsahib English, thought Bhola, as he prepared to cross the road. He wondered if the little Sikh boy had managed to make his way to school.

The lights at the intersection changed to red, and a new row of vehicles came to a standstill. Bhola cleared his throat and prepared to sing, for another round of begging.

The Novice

I

The girls of St Catherine's Convent assembled in straight lines on the quadrangle. The November fog formed a thick spool of cold around the building, and Beena Thomas of Class XI A could barely see the imposing figure of their Principal, Sister Marie Rita Emmanuelle, standing on the podium and testing the microphone that was to broadcast a carefully worded speech. She shivered in the early grey morning but didn't complain about the cold, like the other girls who were buttoning their maroon cardigans and blazers up to the very last button.

Beena was happy to be back in school, surrounded by sleepyheads and squealers, buffoons and beauty queens—her classmates. The ones she would be separated from soon. She knew she would still be attending classes with them, but it wouldn't be the same. She would have to 'maintain a respectable distance', as Sister Emmanuelle had instructed her. Once the convent claimed her, it would dictate her behaviour.

It would draw a meticulous timetable, neatly dividing her hours between prayer and service to the community, for the rest of her life.

She felt the winter morning sting her bare legs and ruffle the layer of down on her skin. Her socks had fallen to her ankles and formed a crinkly ring of warmth. She was wearing a navy-blue skirt a little above her waistline so it fell just above the knees. But it managed to graze them, in a show of modesty that vanished the moment she walked. Her naked limbs, taut with new muscle and rippling with goosebumps, were, at least for the moment, a gentle rebellion against her fate. Soon, she would take her vows and join the congregation of Apostolic Carmelites. Her flesh, with all its tender promise of plumpness here, firmness there, a sudden flare of collarbones and a surprising flash of veins as delicate and fissured as the coastline she belonged to, would lie untouched under the layers of a starchy white habit.

'It is the only way out,' her father Anil Thomas had said, as they had stood by the helm of his old fishing boat. She had come home to her tiny coastal village for the summer vacation and was helping him unload his catch. She had pleaded with him, the red ribbons on her dark braids fluttering in the salty air like flags declaring their youth and autonomy.

'A girl without dowry is no girl, she is spinster,' he had sputtered in a toddy-soaked rage, when she had suggested that she would drop out of school and go fishing with him—learn how to lay the nets and pull the catch out of the water. Her hard work and salesmanship would drive local customers and foreign tourists to their shack by the sea, where Anil Thomas cooked and served a variety of curries. Their 'restha-raunth' could do with a little help from hard-working feminine hands such as hers—she would scrub the floor and buy checked table cloths for the plastic tables that had been placed haphazardly in the shack. Her mother, whom Anil Thomas called the 'mad hag' when he was sober, and a flurry of unmentionable expletives when he was in a toddy swoon, had confined herself to their grubby home a long time ago, cooking meals that reeked with the resentment of a small, unfulfilled life. She emerged only to walk to the market on cooler evenings, when the air wasn't bursting with humidity.

Beena had decided to cook, clean and do whatever it took to swell the family's meagre income and raise a dowry so she could marry a local fisherman. She had instinctively identified one or two suitors—adolescent boys who walked bare-chested through beaches and by-lanes, their gangly arms raised to balance wicker baskets of the day's catch on their heads, their pelvis covered with checked lungis, which set off the cinnamon tone of their bodies.

'Back to school you go, you go now,' Anil Thomas had fumed. No daughter of his was going to spend the rest of her life scraping the scales off catch, removing guts, washing away blood. Instead, she would serve the Church, and get a 'free and decent eddication'. He had spoken to Sister Emmanuelle, who had run a tiny school in the village a long time ago, before she had been transferred to the convent in the city. Beena, who had grown up under Sister Emmanuelle's beady gaze, had been packed off to St Catherine's Convent in New Delhi the moment she hit puberty. Necessary arrangements had been made. Beena was to finish high school, take her vows, and never set foot in the village again.

'A spinster nun is better than a spinster nobody,' he had declared, drinking his milky-white intoxicant.

Now, as she stood on the quadrangle, the memory of that summer filled her with the heat of its intent. Beena Thomas would soon be laid to rest, in her navy-blue skirt and maroon blazer. A 'spinster nun' would take her place during the winter term.

She wanted to hitch her skirt high and dance to the tune of 'Oru Madhurakinavin Lahariyilengo Kudamullapoo Virinju'—the rage in her village currently—in front of the sombre audience of the Special Assembly. She wanted to unbutton her shirt and flash her firm breasts in front of Sister Emmanuelle's overfed face. She wanted to laugh out loud when Mitali Chaudhuri, the senior-school prankster, cracked a silly one.

Instead, she stood with her head hung low, waiting for Sister Emmanuelle to speak into the microphone.

II

A wave of static, amplified by the boxy speakers that stood on the podium on either side of Sister Emmanuelle, filled the air. She touched the microphone lightly with her index finger and said, 'Check one, two, three,' swiftly, before commencing with her speech.

A row of chapped lips broke into giggles at the crackling sound the words made. Beena heard someone whisper, 'Sister Emmanuelle is the same colour as the air.' She guessed it was Mitali Chaudhuri, whose breath was forming a tiny blizzard of cloud and mirth when she spoke.

'I can only see her black veil talking to the mike,' she heard someone else say.

More giggling amongst the rows of students of Class XI A. The girls looked down at the rough sandstone slabs of the quadrangle to keep themselves from being caught and punished in front of the entire school. Beena observed with a sudden panic that the head girl, Shalini Mohan, who stood in the front row, had turned around, sensing a commotion. Her badge, with the words 'Head Girl' embossed in gold, glinted with silent authority as she surveyed the line of students that had dared to talk during the solemn proceedings of the Special Assembly.

Beena singled out Mitali Chaudhuri, whose cheeks rose like mounds of gulab jamun—the one who had probably started the hilarity. Firdaus Nazim stood next to Mitali Chaudhuri, a tittering accomplice, who now studied the laces of her white canvas shoes. Beena wondered if the noise-makers would be punished for not behaving with dignity and decorum in the presence of the Principal. Maybe they would be asked to jog around the school compound two or three times in the freezing cold. Maybe the newly appointed head girl and star pupil of senior school would 'have a word' with their class teacher, Mrs Fernandes. Shalini Mohan's word, with the weight of its office, would convince Mrs Fernandes to give them extra homework that week, or debar them from the school's annual fête, to be attended by the city's biggest educational institutes, including St Joseph's High School, with its crowd of green-blazered boys.

Beena noticed that the junior school sat in neat rows right in front, a few inches away from the podium on which Sister Emmanuelle stood. She wondered if they knew why Sister Emmanuelle had called for a Special Assembly. The senior students were aware of the riot—they had been reading the newspapers and watching the news. The school had closed down for two weeks or so in the middle of the term. A circular, neatly typed by Sister Emmanuelle's secretary, Mrs Hope, had been distributed among the students. It had cited 'extenuating circumstances' as the reason for the unexpected holiday. The school had reopened only a few days ago, after Doordarshan's chiffon-draped newsreader had reassured the city that there were 'no new incidents of violence'. An announcement had been made, through the school's intercom facility, that a Special Assembly would be held soon.

There had been wild speculations on the school bus this morning, especially amongst the girls of junior school. Beena was standing at the back of the bus, listening to the younger ones as they chattered.

'Sister Emmanuelle is happy to see us after the break. That's why there's a Special Assembly today,' Divya Tandon of Class V B suggested, inviting immediate derision from Reema Patel.

'Sister Emmanuelle can *never* be happy about anything. Ever seen her smile? Her face is like a stuffed paratha, with no eyes and no lips. How can she be happy, *ever*?'

Beena had smiled at this somewhat credible explanation of Sister Emmanuelle's persistent unhappiness. She would miss the morning banter on the bus. Once she joined the convent, there would be no more bus rides to school. The convent was within the school compound, and a short walk away from the school building. She would have to move out of her aunt's cramped flat soon. She knew that Usha—her father's sister—was thrilled about her taking her vows this winter. The cranky crone, with her three snotty children and a husband who usually lay around the flat in rum-induced sloth, had not been pleased when Beena had moved in to finish high school in the city. They were getting rid of her, finally. Her own family had connived to imprison her within the whitewashed walls of the convent, resonating with hymns that sickened her with their sweetness.

She had swallowed the lump in her throat and stared out of the bus window. The eucalyptus trees that lined the roads had loomed before her, dark and unkempt, stunned into silence by what they had recently witnessed. There were quite a few vehicles on the road, but they drove cautiously, as though frightened by what might be waiting for them as they turned a corner, or stood at a red light.

'Where's Amrit Kaur?' Divya Tandon asked.

'She's not in the bus today,' a classmate replied.

Probably at home, where it's safe, Beena had thought, as she saw that a scooter had collapsed on the road, its front tyre a flaming halo that was expanding rapidly. The smell of melting rubber drifted into the bus, and some of the students placed their handkerchiefs on their noses. A junior rubbed her eyes and started to wail. So the lady in pink chiffon, who read the news on Doordarshan, had been wrong about the city calming down. Why the great hurry to open the school, what if something happened to us now, she had thought bitterly, as the bus made its way through familiar streets which had grown eerily strange over the past few days, towards school.

III

The speech fluttered in Sister Emmanuelle's hand now, but she barely referred to it. She has probably learnt it by heart, thought Beena. She looked in the direction of the podium and saw that Sister Emmanuelle's eyes were fixed on her. She looked away, her brown skin bristling with fear. The Principal's voice reverberated through the winter morning.

> '*We are gathered here to pray for harmony in this beautiful city that has recently witnessed...a brief disturbance.*'

Beena felt a nerve grow taut on her forehead, and twitch in silent anger. To call the murder of a Prime Minister by her own Sikh bodyguards, and the riot that it had triggered, 'a brief disturbance' was to deliberately underplay the events of the past few weeks. What if the rioters had killed the father, or grandfather, or an uncle of a Sikh student of this school? Had Sister Emmanuelle bothered to find out if *all* the students had returned to school, and that nothing untoward had happened to any Sikh family? Or maybe—Beena was willing to feel slightly charitable towards the nun who would soon become her novice guardian—she didn't want to mention the unpleasant details of the riot because it would upset the junior students.

'Let us be grateful to the Lord, and sing His praise…'

The Choral Society walked noiselessly to the podium and stood in a group, preparing to sing a hymn the moment Sister Emmanuelle concluded her speech.

'Let us pray to Him, for the protection of…'

Sister Emmanuelle's sentence formed irregular syllables of cold breath and hung in the air, unfinished. She stared at the wrought-iron gates of the school, which had creaked suddenly, disrupting the Special Assembly. The students turned around collectively, as the gates opened. Someone walked in—her long braids swinging as she took a few steps, a schoolbag slung across one shoulder and a water bottle across another. She turned around to wave goodbye to a couple in a white Fiat, which drove off the moment she was inside the gates.

'Amrit Kaur of II A!' Beena muttered. 'She wasn't on the bus today.'

The little girl froze when she saw that the entire school was staring at her.

'You're late!' Sister Emmanuelle's voice boomed through the microphone. Amrit Kaur stood rooted to a sandstone tile, her face puckering with snot and shameful tears before the Special Assembly. But Shalini Mohan reached the spot where the girl stood, and gently led her to where her class was seated.

'At least now we know that *everyone* is here,' grinned Beena to herself, as Sister Emmanuelle continued to speak into the microphone.

The Prisoner

Balbir ji STOP Come quickly STOP I am hurt STOP

If I could send you telegrams from here, I would send you one every day. There is so much I have to tell you. I have to share this lock-up with pickpockets, throat-cutters, ganja-and charas-sellers, randis. I have to clean the latrines. Everyone in the lock-up has loose motions. Sometimes they vomit in the latrine too. The food here is not good.

You were always so kind to me. You always shared your chole-chawal, kadhi-chawal, rajma-chawal with me. You always said, 'Puttar, you are a bachelor, share my food, puttar.' You always said, 'When you find yourself a wife then you can bring me lunch from your new home, cooked by your wife's soft and loving hands.' You always said you will always be there for me.

Balbir ji STOP Help me STOP

How long has it been? Has it been a week or a month? I am unwell. I have to scrape and scrape the toilets clean every day. Every day, I have to clean and clean with a bottle of phenyl. Come quickly. I am hurt. Sometimes when I'm scraping and cleaning, I pick up the bottle of phenyl and read what is written on the orangey glass: POISONOUS. NOT TO BE TAKEN. I pick up the bottle and I think: what if I take it? If I drink the entire bottle, will they miss it? If I drink the entire bottle, will they miss me? If I drink the entire bottle, will you come quickly?

The riot is over. I heard the news on the radio. The SHO was listening to the radio, his legs on a table full of files, his fingers around a glass of tea. The radio made a sound like oil when it is heated. When the noise of oil inside the radio became soft, I heard a voice. That voice told all the officers and all the criminals of Punjabi Bagh Police Thana that the riot was over. I can't remember how many days have passed since I heard the news. The radio has been removed from the police station. The police doesn't want the prisoners to know what is going on outside. The lock-up is the only world I know now. Cleaning the latrines is the only work I do now. My hands, which once held only soft Pashminas, brocades and silks in your store, now hold latrine brushes and chemical cleaners.

But why lie? Why lie about what my hands have known and what they have not? If my hands were innocent, they would not have known the cold steel of handcuffs. If my hands were without sin, they would not have known the thrill of holding a pistol. If my hands were innocent, they would not have pulled the trigger.

Balbir ji STOP Come quickly STOP Someone is waiting STOP

I am engaged, Balbir ji. I was going to tell you that very soon I would bring my own tiffin box to the store, but the Prime Minister was murdered. The roka ceremony had to be postponed. I am engaged. Am I still engaged? Why couldn't the Prime Minister get killed after my roka ceremony? My hands were meant to know what many hands in filmy songs know. Fingertips touching fingertips. Fingers locked together around a bottle of Gold Spot. Fingers tracing the outline of red lips. Palms around heart-shaped faces. My hands were meant to do what Amitabh and Shashi and Rishi and Jeetendra do to Rekha and Jaya and Rakhi and Dimple. My hands were not meant to scrub toilets. My hands were not meant to dangle from the space between the iron bars of the lock-up, begging to be set free.

I am not a criminal STOP Come quickly STOP

She is waiting for me. I know she is waiting for me. She is the type of girl who waits silently. Even inside the store, where I first saw her, she was waiting silently. She was standing in front of a row of silk spools. She was standing with a girl who looked very well-fed. That girl, I came to know later, was her best friend from The Lady Edwina Home Economics Institute. They were shopping together for some silk fabric. The very well-fed girl had unrolled the spools of shocking pink, sunshine yellow, and flame-of-the-forest orange silk fabric. The very well-fed girl had draped the fabric around her heavy shoulders. The very well-fed girl was standing in a jumble of pink-yellow-orange when I saw the mess. I had to leave an elderly couple who were trying on Angora wool sweaters, and rush to where the very well-fed girl was standing, with *her,* my to-be fiancé. She stood quietly, watching her friend hold the colours against her skin. She stretched out her slender arms, now and then, to help her friend with the rustling material.

'Try the jacquard,' she said, in a voice sweet like Phantom cigarettes. 'The magenta Benarsi is too gaudy,' she said in her Ravalgon voice.

I walked through the swelling reams of cloth. Slowly, I folded the heap of cloth around the very-well-fed girl. 'I am here to assist you, bhenji,' I said to her, politely but firmly. 'Anything you want, you just ask me, bhenji,' I said. 'No need to unroll the fabric on your own, bhenji,' I told her. And then, slowly, very slowly, I turned around to *her,* my silent to-be fiancé. 'Have you been waiting for someone to show you the material?' I asked without looking at her. I did not wait for a reply (what if she said 'No, I'm not waiting; I'm just here to help my friend make up her mind'). I simply pulled out a roll of firoza-blue raw silk. The fabric opened out like the blue waters of the Beas. 'Firoza silk,' I said to her. 'It will suit you so much, Miss…aahaha…Miss…'

'Chandrika,' she said, looking at the fabric, not at me.

'Chandrika,' I said. 'Miss Chandrika, if you get a kameez stitched with this firoza silk, you will look like a…like a…

ahhhummm...pink rose blooming in the garden...a...a pink rose...with a summery sky in the background...'

I spoke to her like a schoolboy with marbles in his mouth. What if she thought I was a smooth-like-Amul-butter salesman? What if she thought I was making a sales pitch with my not-so-original comparisons? What if she thought that comparing her to a pink rose was not a sincere compliment?

She was blushing. 'Miss Chandrika,' I said, still looking at the firoza fabric. 'Get the kameez cut in Saira Banu style...it will hug your fine figure when you walk...' She giggled. Her friend hmphed. Her friend had the figure of Tun Tun and could never wear a kameez cut in Saira-Banu style. Her friend, who was feeling ignored, nudged her, my pink rose.

'It is almost lunch time,' she said. 'If you are serious about the firoza-shiroza, then tell him to cut three-and-a-half metres,' she ordered. 'Then let's go to Nathu's for chole-bhature,' she hissed.

Chandrika giggled, and it sounded like ghungroos tinkling. She held the firoza-blue silk between her long fingers. She said to the fabric, 'Kindly cut the material.' Her voice was soft ripples of velvet; her diction a delight. I measured the fabric and cut it. 'Thank you,' she said.

'Hmmmmph!' said her friend. 'I'm the one who needs material for a suit, and *you're* the one doing all the shopping,' she whined.

Balbir ji STOP Chandrika and I are to be married STOP

My Chandrika is waiting for me. We used to meet every day. After that day in the shop, we met outside the gates of her institute. After that day in the shop, we met wherever it was possible to meet in Delhi. Underneath the gulmohar trees outside her institute, which rained flowers on us as we gazed at each other. At Keventer's, for milk in foreign flavours—she drank one whole litre of strawberry, and I, butterscotch. At Nirula's, where we went round and round the rotating doors and were dizzy by the time our Hot Chocolate Fudge came. At Regal Cinema, for a show. In the lawns around India Gate, sharing a newspaper cone full of chana-chor-garam. Under a harshingar tree in Lodhi Garden, where I lay with my head on her lap. We met every day. I want to meet her soon. I want to meet her now.

Delhi is no longer under curfew. A beat constable was telling the SHO that there is traffic on the roads. School buses are full of children who must be going to school after weeks of sitting at home. City babus must be beep-beeping their way to work in their white Ambassadors. Connaught Place must be open for business. Candy-floss walas and balloon-walas must be selling their wares at crossings and junctions. The sweepers would have scrubbed the bloodstains off the roads, the galis, the pavements, the intersections. The kadamb, shahtoot and jamun trees, which have seen everything, will never speak. The leper, who lives inside an Onida TV cardboard box on the footpath, will never speak. The dog that howls at passers-by, with stories of who-killed-who and with what, will never speak. Balbir ji, will you never speak?

Riot over STOP Release me STOP

The city has lost its patience with the dying and the dead. This crazy city has quickly forgotten the murders. It has moved on. It is on the move. Balbir ji, press the choke of your Premier Padmini and be on the move. Tell them to set me free. If you don't, then who will? I am hurt.

My parents are old. Have you told them I am in jail? Has someone told them I am alive but in jail? My parents need me. My father is a heart patient. He used to be a halwai. He has spent his whole life frying samosas and making jalebis. He has spent his whole life stirring deep pans that spat oil on his face. He has spent his whole life curdling milk into rabri and kheer. I am the son of a halwai. I am the son of a halwai; I became a store assistant and a criminal. I should have become a doctor. I almost became a doctor. A few days before the medical entrance exam, I fell ill. 'Typhoid,' Dr Tripathi (MBBS, MD) said. 'Must be the bad food and water,' he said, pressing his stethoscope into my hairless chest. 'Do you boil your water?' he asked my mother. He was staring and staring at the damp patches on the walls and ceilings. The damp patches had formed maps of new countries on the walls and ceilings. Dr Tripathi was staring and staring at the damp maps. Maybe he is trying to name them, I had thought. Maybe he will call them Venezuelan Hemorrhagic Fever, Tinea Corporis, Pertussis. I had memorized the names of 216 infectious diseases for my medical entrance exam. 'Boil your drinking water,' Dr Tripathi said to my mother. 'And try and keep the kitchen clean,' he scolded. My mother nodded. Dr Tripathi left with the stethoscope dangling around his neck.

I was too sick to take the exam. I had to do my B Com. through correspondence. I had to become a store assistant. There was no other way. The only options were to become a store assistant or a halwai assistant. I used to work with my father during my B Com-through-correspondence days. If you, Balbir ji, had not been sitting on that broken wooden bench in my father's dhaba, I would still be serving kulfis. If you, Balbir ji, had not noticed my Character, Courtesy, Cleanliness (the Three Cs that dangle from a laminated notice above the cashier's counter in Balbir & Sons) on that day, I would still be a halwai's assistant. If I had become a halwai's assistant, I would still be a free man. If I had become a halwai assistant, I would not have pulled the trigger.

Parents are old STOP They will worry STOP Come quickly STOP

How will you manage without me, Balbir ji? You always said the store was full of customers because of me. You always said it was my Colgate smile. You always said I could sell yards of rose pink, carnation pink, blushing-bride pink and baby's-bottom pink all in one day and sometimes to the same person. You always said it was the way I unrolled the fabric, like I was a merchant from the Arabian Nights, selling magic carpets. You always said it was my voice—soothing like a lullaby, hypnotic like the tunes of a snake-charmer. Now all I do is clean the latrines of Punjabi Bagh Thana. Now all I do is wait. Wait for more news, whispered between constables, overheard by convicts, through the bars of the lock-up. Wait for you, Balbir ji. Wait for my Chandrika. Wait for someone to come and set me free. I am a store assistant. The son of a halwai. The fiancé of an MSc. in Home Economics. I am not a criminal.

Every day, the inmates of Punjabi Bagh Thana stand in a row and sing 'Aye malik tere bande hum'. We pray to whichever god we have strayed away from. Aye Ram, Aye Rahim, Aye Yeshu Masih, we are your people. We pray to seek the light that has gone out, like a fused ECE bulb. We pray to read the holy books. We pray for the souls of those whose throats we have slit, or wallets we have picked. We pray to think good, to do good, to speak good. Aye Ram, Aye Rahim, Aye Yeshu Masih, we pray that we may never stray.

And then, in the night, we do good to each other. We practise what we sing and what we recite. We do good to each other. With our calloused hands. Backwards and forwards, again and again. The inmate doing good and the inmate receiving good both grunt like pigs. I have been grunting for a week. I have told them that I am engaged, but still the inmates do good to me. I told them Chandrika won't like me if I tell her you have done good to me. They don't stop. They say my bottom is like an unripe aloo-bukhara. Smooth and hairless. The inmates don't use Vaseline. In the morning we pray and in the night we do good to each other. They do good to me, sometimes three or four times. If you don't come quickly I will drink the full bottle of phenyl. If you don't come quickly, you will lose your store assistant.

Urgent STOP They do good to me STOP I am hurt STOP

I was assisting you till the police came and took me away. If I hadn't pushed you inside your teakwood cabinet full of Pashmina, you would have been killed. The rioters had broken into the store. They had set our plastic family on fire. Do you remember the mannequins in the display window, Balbir ji? The daddy-mummy-child that we had dressed up together in new woollens? That family melted and burned together. They were made of plastic and nylon, but I know the child mannequin was very scared before it died. The paint on its face dripped like black-white-red tears. The flames caught the pom-poms on its woollen cap, and its crimson lips twisted and let out a scream. I heard the child mannequin scream. I heard daddy and mummy mannequin sing a last lullaby to their burning plastic baby. I heard the rioters shout 'Sardar ka bachcha, murdabad.' I saw them break the glass on the doors and windows of the store. I saw them pull out the fabric—from shelves and drawers, from cupboards and cabinets—and soak yards and yards of cloth in kerosene. At any moment, they would have pulled you out of the Pashmina cabinet. At any moment, they would have wrapped you in Pashmina and poured a jerry can of fuel on you. At any moment, you would have burned with hand-embroidered chinar leaves and paisleys around your shoulders.

I knew about the pistol in the cashier's drawer. I had seen you put it there. I never asked you where it came from. I thought your cousin Jaspreet had given it to you. I knew you would never use it to kill anyone. It's probably there to scare the pigeons that have built a nest on the new signage 'Balbir & Sons', I had thought. You had painted the signage yourself. You hated those pigeons.

'They are trespasser pigeons,' you had said. Their droppings would slide down the signage and streak the lettering. 'People will think Balbir & Sons is run by a family of zebras,' you had joked.

Balbir ji STOP Talk to police STOP I used pistol in self-defense STOP

I only used your pistol to scare the rioters away. I had to use it. They would have burnt down Balbir & Sons. They would have killed me, even though I am not a sardar. I told them I was not a sardar. I told them…I told them I was just a store assistant. A Hindu, just like them. They were moving closer and closer to me. Those angry men with jerry cans. Angry with all the other sardars who were alive and quietly running their shops, or sliding under the body of an old Fiat to see why it wouldn't start, or sitting at the teller's counter inside a bank, or taking a morning walk or…I only used the pistol when I thought I was going to die. I didn't mean to kill anybody. It was a mistake.

Everything happened so quickly. There was a commotion and I pulled the trigger. I saw that someone fell down. I pulled the trigger and the police came. Why didn't the police come earlier? Why didn't the police come when the rioters came? Why didn't the police arrest the men with lathis? Why didn't the police arrest those who shouted 'Sardar ka bachcha, murdabad'? Why did the police wait for me to pull the trigger before it arrived? I am not a criminal.

If I drink the full bottle of phenyl I will no longer be under arrest. If you, Balbir ji, come quickly, I will no longer be under arrest.

All I do is clean latrines. All I do is wait. All I do is pick lice from the heads of the other prisoners. I pick lice and they do good to me. I tell them 'Don't do good to me; do good to each other.' I tell them, 'I will pick your lice and clean your shit; ph…ah…phleease don't do…aye Ram, aye Rahim…aye Yeshu Masih…save me…ph…do…n..uh…please…no…god… good to me, I…I am en…eng…engaged…pl…ph…ph…don't do good to me…'

Balbir ji STOP I am serious STOP I will drink phenyl STOP

I don't know if you will ever read these telegrams. I have booked these telegrams in my head. The thump-thump of brass on brass is in my head. The tak-tak of the date stamp is in my head. I punch the keys in my head when I clean the latrines. I type the messages in my head when they do good to me. I book my telegrams when I pick lice.

Thump-thump. Tak-tak. Thump-thump. Tak-tak.

The clang-clang of the tele-printer typing my messages is in my head. What is the date today? What was the date yesterday? How does it matter? These telegrams will never reach you. No one in Punjabi Bagh will be shocked by the arrival of so many telegrams. They will fall like leaves that the trees do not want, on the shops and houses. They will drip down from telephone wires and balcony railings, like winter dew. They will cover the roads and pavements like sticky tar. But Punjabi Bagh will not notice. News of me will never be heard outside this police station.

You will never receive the bad news that I am hurt. You will never receive the good news that I am no more.

Maybe they will find the roll of paper in my head when I collapse. Maybe they will read my messages after I have drunk the bottle of phenyl. When I lie in the latrine, with a crack in my skull, or when I faint in the lock-up, with a bleeding aloo-bukhara backside, my telegrams will drop out of my skull, for you to read.

Balbir ji STOP Come quickly STOP Kabir is dead STOP

The Minaret

I

Spring was upon them. Pollinators sucked at anthers; pigeons sat upon pigeons; stray dogs mounted the bitch population of entire streets; monkeys touched themselves; the koel announced its ecstasy in long cries. The silk cotton trees heaved red flowers; swollen beehives hung from its branches. The day was clammy with honey scents. Jaspreet Singh wasn't sure if Amrit was aware of what was on display on that quiet road that led from their home to Chor Minar. He hoped not. He hoped she had not picked up on the sex education VHS that the musky season was playing in slow motion that afternoon.

He was savouring it all—the unhurried walk to Chor Minar with Amrit; the smell of new grass and animals in heat that wafted around him and made his nostrils flare; the sunshine, still mellow from a receding winter, but spiked with rays so warm that they foretold a long summer. Jaspreet was grateful for the warmth. He wanted to put the winter behind him, quicker than the season was allowing him to. He wanted to go on endless walks with Amrit.

The winter had kept him indoors. He had not met his friends in the neighbourhood with the frequency that was vital to his well-being. He had, against the wishes of his family, and the threats of his wife Kulwanti Kaur, met his old gang once or twice at their usual spot under the mulberry tree. He had ventured out soon after Lala Kanshi Chand's barsati was burned down, soon after *he* was made to hide in Major Budhwar's vegetable garden on the night the rioters arrived here, in this quiet lane, which was protected from the menace of the world only by bougainvillea, eucalyptus, neem, and silk cotton trees.

It had been a rushed, uneasy meeting. Gone was the boisterous laughter that could drown out even the cawing of crows. Gone was the hissing and mocking of one another's attempts to exercise. The neighbours had huddled under the tree. One never knew where the rioters would arrive next, they had whispered to one another. The Prime Minister's body lay in a gun carriage in Teen Murti Bhavan, and a grieving city had taken revenge during the days meant for silence and mourning. Young Gursimran would have died in that barsati with his wife, had Ram Narayan Khanna not taken them in. No, no, Mr Singh should not be seen in the park, he should sit at home, why is he here, didn't Doordarshan warn him about stray incidents of violence?

So he had stayed at home for the rest of winter, huddled on the dewan in front of his Texla colour TV, which conveyed the news through the rosebud lips of a newscaster whose sari always matched the colour of the flower in her hair.

Jaspreet was grateful he was alive; a silly disguise had cheated death, and here he was, walking with Amrit in early spring. The disguise had been created by Amrit, and Sweetie, who they were about to meet in Chor Minar. The girls had thought he was playing a game of face-painting to look like the scariest gods and goddesses they had seen inside the temple near Chor Minar. They had painted thick black strokes around his eyes. They had asked him to stick his tongue out and had splashed crimson on it from a gleaming Camlin paint box. His turban had been removed, and his hair, rolled tightly into a bun, had been uncoiled. He was Ma Kali, fearsome in every way but for the strands of silver in the thick dark hair cascading down to touch his knees, which Amrit had suggested they paint a jet black, because how could Ma Kali, who killed bad people, be as old as Dadaji?

Amrit and Sweetie had saved him that night, although they didn't know it. There was so much they didn't know, these almost-six-year-olds; there was so much he wanted them to know. But he would have to wait. He would have to wait for many seasons to come and go before he could tell them a story unlike any other they had heard from him: once upon a time, a Prime Minister ordered her army to enter a temple. She was looking for a man, a man with a gun, whom some called Sant. Her army killed many people that summer; they were praying with their heads bowed inside the Harmandir

Sahib, and couldn't escape when the gunshots rang out. Her army killed the man with the gun as well, but so many good people, who were there only to recite the Gurbani, died along with him, that it was decided that very summer, that the Prime Minister too would have to die. And so it came to be, that summer turned to winter and the Prime Minister also died, shot by her own bodyguards. And that winter, your Dadaji was almost killed. But a cunning plan to hide him had been hatched by all the grown-ups, and you clever children had painted his face, and he had stood in Major Budhwar's garden, absolutely still, for he was Kali the scarecrow; he was Kali the protector of fruit and vegetables; he was Kali the tormentor of evil crows and pigeons and cheels. The rioters had gone away, fooled by Kali, who never blinked when a light hit his face, and they all lived happily ever after.

No, not everyone lived happily ever after. If Jaspreet was some day going to tell this story to the girls, and especially to his Amrit, whom he knew would ask a lot of questions, he would have to tell it with honesty. He would have to bring up Block 32—not here, but there, on the other side of the river—Block 32 had grown cold and silent. 'Why Dadaji?' he wanted Amrit to ask when she was older, 'Why did Block 32 grow silent? Why did all the men disappear? When did the wailing stop?' He would tell her, he would tell her everything. He wouldn't leave out the burning tyres they flung around the men of Block 32, or the cans of petrol they poured on someone's father and someone's husband, or the little boys, whose hair was braided so that they looked like little girls when they ran with their mothers, far, far away from their homes, which had gone up in flames that bellowed in the skies for days.

He wanted Amrit, clasping his fingers now, and pulling his hand so that he walked a little faster, to grow up quickly, and want, no, *need* to know. 'Why is Balbir Chacha always so sad?' he wanted her to ask him, 'And where is Kabir Bhaiya?' There was no news of Kabir, and Jaspreet wondered if there ever would be. His cousin Balbir Singh's shop in Punjabi Bagh had been looted and set on fire. The shop's young assistant, Kabir, had been arrested by the police, for shooting at the rioters who had broken into the shop. Kabir had tried to disperse the crowd, he had probably only wanted to scare them away—Jaspreet was sure of that—but he had accidentally killed a rioter. The police arrived after the shop had been plundered and gutted, and took Kabir away. No one had heard of him after that, even though Balbir and Jaspreet had gone to the Punjabi Bagh Police Station and tried to bail him out.

Would Amrit grow up curious enough, and angry enough, to some day go through all the FIRs, neatly filed in the Punjabi Bagh station, and find one about the looting of Balbir & Sons? Was there an FIR or even a warrant of arrest that permitted the police to detain poor Kabir? If Amrit never found one, she would know that Kabir had been unlawfully arrested... she would know...she would know that he had probably died in prison, beaten by the cops who had not caught or sent to prison a single rioter on that day.

Jaspreet wanted to howl like Amrit did when a bedtime story was left unfinished. His face prickled and felt hot; the sharp odours that had teased him moments ago now smelt like rotting flesh. Should he turn around…he wasn't feeling too well…would he live long enough to tell Amrit everything that was choking him up right now?

'Amrrrrit!' The cry was impatient but happy. Sweetie. She let go of Major Budhwar's hand and hopped-skipped-jumped towards her friend. Together, the girls ran up a short flight of stairs, carved in stone on a circular elevation that surrounded Chor Minar.

Of what use are an old man's morose thoughts to children? Let them play, Jaspreet snuffled, there will be time enough to dwell on the dead.

II

If Chor Minar's cylindrical minaret could speak, it would probably complain about the many outrages it withstood every day, thought Jaspreet as he slowly climbed up the stairs with Major Budhwar. The tower that once struck terror in the ancient capital of Siri was now a place of recreation, and worse, for the many pigeons that had built nests in the holes on the face of the minaret, a place of procreation. The holes were meant for the decapitated heads of thieves to dangle from, during the reign of that relentless collector of offending heads, Ala-ud-din Khilji. But that was in the thirteenth century.

Today, Frisbees, shuttlecocks and cricket balls whizzed past these holes, disturbing beheaded phantoms whose shrieks one could hear if one climbed the spiral staircase inside Chor Minar, which led to to its uneven roof. Droppings of all varieties—bats, rodents, pregnant birds—slithered down the face of the minaret, and made whoever dared to enter the monument slip into a marsh of faeces.

The locals were not afraid of the ghosts of Khilji's empire, though. They climbed the broken steps all the time, to get to the roof and to sit there for a while for an aerial view of the neighbourhood and its familiar inhabitants. How thrilling, for adolescent climbers, to view the preparations for a birthday party they were not invited to—crates of Campa Cola and Gold Spot being lifted out of the dickie of a Premier Padmini or a Contessa, by a khansama; packets of paper streamers being scotch-taped in loops on the walls and ceiling of the verandah; a khoi bag stuffed with Kismi toffees, 5 Star chocolates, plastic whistles, pencils, erasers, and other treasures being hoisted on the ceiling, to be broken after the cake was cut.

There were other affronts to the monument's once formidable stature. Post-pubescent couples pecked at each other in its many alcoves, or smoked Charminar cigarettes in the solitude of the minaret's long shadows, which protected them from the prying eyes of grandparents taking a stroll, or family ayahs gossiping with each other as they walked with tin containers full of frothy milk from the DMS booth, or the postman who came daily, ringing the bell of his Atlas cycle to announce the arrival of aerograms, money orders, and telegrams. The dread that Chor Minar once evoked had been replaced by indifference.

'If ghosts could speak, they would tell us to get the hell out of here,' said Jaspreet to Major Budhwar, who was staring at the holes on the minaret. New nests had appeared in several of them; broken eggs leaked stillborn birds onto the façade. They were standing in the small park that surrounded Chor Minar. The grass was long and almost grazed their knees. No mali has been here since last summer, thought Jaspreet, walking towards an alcove.

'Let's not speak of ghosts, Mr Singh, let's not speak of ghosts. Dilli is full of them; thank your lucky stars…or your Guru…*and my* cabbage patch that you are standing here in flesh and blood,' said Major Budhwar, pinching the soft mounds of Jaspreet's cheeks when he said flesh and blood.

'Major Saab, I owe you, and your bloody cabbage patch, my life. But…but…don't stop an old man like me from going on and on about ghosts.' Jaspreet paused and inhaled the pungent grassy air before continuing, 'I was…we were… we were so fond of Kabir, Major Saab…and no one knows anything about him…it has been three months…' Jaspreet felt his eyes fill with embarrassing tears. He turned his face away from his neighbour and blinked furiously at an alcove until the tears subsided.

'We will find a way, Mr Singh…we will find a way to get Kabir out…if he is still alive.' Major Budhwar spoke in a tone softer than the one he used when he baby-talked his sweet-pea tendrils.

'He is dead…I know it…otherwise why would the police say "There is no one by the name of Kabir Duggal here in this thana," when Balbir and I went looking for him? He is dead, Major Saab, beaten to death in the lock-up…no report against him…no case…just arrest and then puf! he disappears…'

'If anyone should be dead, it is those bastards in white kurta-pyjamas…those party workers who held rallies and handed out lathis and sariyas to the stupid public and told them to kill, kill, kill every single sardar man. If I could slit the throat of those politicians, I would Mr Singh, their heads would hang from Chor Minar for all to see…they are the real murderers, Mr Singh…sitting fat in their living rooms, serving the new Prime Minister…if I could behead them, Mr Singh…'

Jaspreet put his arm around Major Budhwar's drooping shoulders and coaxed him into silence. He didn't want the old Major to get too excited; he was here for whatever comfort the warmer season could provide. Together, they walked through the tangle of grass and weed to a flowering champa tree. Amrit and Sweetie sat under it. They held something between their muddy fingers—an old cloth which they were about to fold. It was long but tattered. Jaspreet bent down for a closer look.

'Dadaji, look at this old chunni…which aunty left it here?' Amrit asked Jaspreet, who took the cloth in his hands.

'It's not a chunni, it's a sari for the fairy who lives on the tree,' Sweetie chirruped, holding it a little higher for Major Budhwar to examine. He grunted at his granddaughter and turned his attention to the burnished green leaves of the champa.

'It's dirty…it's so brown-brown…and it has a beard,' Amrit laughed.

'How can a sari have a beard?' Sweetie giggled.

Jaspreet saw the beard. Clumps of hair sticking together in blobs of congealed blood. He snatched the cloth from the girls and stumbled towards Major Budhwar.

They stared at it in silence before they let it fall onto the grass.

'Wahe Guru!' Jaspreet whispered, 'Whose turban lies here? Whose murder does it scream of? How many…ho…how… man…many more sardars will have to die…Wahe Guru… tell me…'

Jaspreet stood under the champa and held onto a branch, his body swaying. He looked up at the holes that pockmarked Chor Minar. 'How many heads…how many good…no… nob…noble heads will have to bleed for the sake of one Prime Minister?' he sputtered, his body dropping to the ground, before Major Budhwar caught him.

Weakly, he clung to Major Budhwar and gazed at Amrit and Sweetie, standing at the spot where they had found the turban. They held hands; Sweetie was also twisting and untwisting the lacy edges of her frock. They should be home, what are they doing here…Hai Rabba! Why did we come here today… is there no rest for me…why…oh why… why am I not dead, thought Jaspreet, leaning against his friend as they staggered towards the grandchildren.

BOOK II

Old Bones

I

Kulwanti Kaur, who lay in the intensive care unit of a private hospital, could hear the sound of wailing as she drifted in and out of consciousness.

Kulwanti knew that death was received with high decibels in this hospital, and everywhere else in this city. It was only fitting to send near-and-dear ones, now stiff and cold, their bodies covered with a white cloth speckled with garlands, to the cremation grounds after a crowd of inconsolable mourners had beaten their chests, torn their hair out with their fingernails, and swayed back and forth with arms flailing in every direction. She hoped that the news of her death would cause enough tears to dampen the aquamarine walls of this hospital, and stir up the topography of other lifelines threatening to flatten. They should know—those who slept fitfully after a long and complex surgery, and those who lay awake in a pool of pain—that she, Kulwanti Kaur, had been snuffed out by a bout of pneumonia. A bitter wind, and an insolent faith that her strong sardarni genes could withstand anything, let alone the onset of a chill, had reduced her plump body to a skeleton on life support. A skeleton whose diamond nose–pin glinted through the oxygen mask on her face—she knew it shone as brilliantly now as it did then, when she first wore it as a young bride of sixteen. A tiny sphere of light, defying the doctor's verdict.

All that was left of her was a heap of old bones. And a pair of blue-grey eyes, the colour of a Peshawar sky, refusing to shut in spite of the heavy dose of sedatives, trying to glare back at the nurse or doctor who peered at her face every now and then, to let them know she was furious about having her veins pierced by their needles.

Several thoughts crossed her drugged mind during her bouts of wakefulness. For one, she felt like tearing off the oxygen mask and bombarding the staff in intensive care with her favourite Punjabi cusswords. Who was that marjani in the white skirt-and-blouse who had dared to tighten the mask around her face? She had probably created permanent grooves on Kulwanti's translucent complexion, and just for that, the khasma-nu-khani deserved to die. And these wristbands restraining her arms. Why couldn't she remove the oxygen mask herself; she was certain it was because her arms had been tied to the bed. That khote-da-puttar in dirty green pyjamas had tied her up. Good for him, she thought through the painkiller-induced sloth, or his baby cheeks would've known the sting of a sardarni's slap.

Kulwanti wasn't meant to die on a narrow bed in intensive

care. She was meant to die as vividly as she had lived. To succumb to a bout of pneumonia, her veins swollen with antibiotics, was a wishy-washy conclusion to a life lived with flair. Groggily, she wondered if this battle with a fancy congestion was worth it. Maybe she should just let go; instruct that moron in green overalls to sever the tubes and invite death with her usual enthusiasm for newness.

Like that winter afternoon in 1950, not long after the country had been partitioned, and Hindus and Muslims had been surgically separated by makers of nation states. She had invited Begum Tabassum Bano for a cup of tea and some pakodas. Begum Tabassum Bano was from the only Muslim family in the lane canopied with amaltas and gulmohar trees, in which Kulwanti lived. The wife of a dry-fruit merchant, who, according to the collective whisperings of the ladies of the neighbourhod, 'travelled far and wide, to Afghanistan and other junglee places, gathering nuts and raisins', Begum Tabassum Bano often found herself alone over long stretches of winter. Kulwanti, intrigued by the blackness of the hijab that covered her head and marked her for isolation in a colony of coiffured rummy-playing ladies, invited her home. That new friendship, conducted over long walks under the ruby shade of gulmohar trees, and across chrysanthemum-lined fences in the colony, was Kulwanti's gregarious rebellion against her eau-de-cologne clan. It was also her defiance of the Partition.

'You can divide countries, but how dare you divide two housewives sharing pain and pakodas,' she would muse, as Begum Tabassum Bano helped herself to a batter-fried filigree of spinach. Kulwanti would then heave her bosom and demarcate a portion of her cleavage to indicate where the pain of being the wife of a busy civil engineer, and the mother of three 'bad rowdies' was emanating from.

She would invite death like she had invited Begum Tabassum Bano—free of suspicion and expecting only the dousing of her need for newness. She would call out to that marjani in the white skirt-and-blouse, and instruct her to remove the oxygen mask. It wasn't her way to meet a new friend with a face that looked older than her eighty-seven years.

She wondered what would become of her beloved make-up kit—the vanity box that her husband had bought her soon after he graduated from engineering college in Punjab University. She had just turned sixteen; he was twenty-one. Their marriage had been arranged by their families, and he had given her the vanity box on the condition that she would learn the multiplication tables (up to fifteen), and recite them in front of him whenever they met. Their courtship was a series of classes, conducted under the bemused gaze of a Delhi twilight. She would stand on the flat roof of her father's house, reciting, 'One twos are two, two twos are four, three twos are six…' as he towered over her, a lanky Sikh boy with a luxuriant beard. He would prompt her by miming the numbers every time she faltered. And whenever she managed to recite an entire table without making mistakes or using her fingers to count the correct answers, he would kiss her gently, on her closed but crimson lips.

The vanity box was hardly used in the first flush of her

married life. Her cheeks were prone to blushing and her husband's sudden embraces made sure they were a natural pink most of the time. It was only later, in the years when a consortium of rummy-playing housewives was formed to resist the drowsiness of long afternoons, that she dabbed a bit of rouge on her cheeks and deepened the colour of her lips with red lipstick. A touch of glamour, as suggested by *Eve's Weekly*, the new magazine she read like a challenging English textbook, underlining words like bouffant and pinafore in an attempt to expand her vocabulary of 'foreign' words whose meanings only her learned husband knew.

Those were happy afternoons, she thought now, as she breathed laboriously through the oxygen mask. The ladies wore either chiffon or silk, depending on the season. The summer was doused with a gigantic cooler in Kulwanti's verandah. Its metallic blades ripped the sloth-heavy air and infused it with the fragrance of khus. The ladies, their wits thus cooled, played a devious game of rummy—shuffling and dealing like knaves, cheating like hardboiled professionals.

The winter games were interspersed with ginger-flavoured tea, swirling in bone-china teacups with lacy floral patterns. Kulwanti tried to trace her lips with her tongue, searching for the mild, lingering flavour of her last cup of tea—was it a day ago, or a week? She couldn't tell. Her tongue felt like the furry coat her husband Jaspreet Singh had bought for her when he had visited London, a long time ago.

She couldn't move her tongue. But she could summon to her mind a blurry image of the rummy players, draped in

Pashmina shawls, (she in her fur coat), sitting on wicker chairs in her garden. Amid rows of dahlias, poppies and Rangoon creepers, they would perform their cunning until rows of approaching headlights in the premature dusk reminded them of their husbands' imminent return from work.

There was one rummy season—she couldn't remember the year—that had been interrupted. Someone important had been murdered—or ass-ass-inated—her Jaspreet had added a new word to her exotic jumble, while explaining to her why he was so glued to the television set. She had thought it was the pretty newsreader with the gigantic rose stuck behind her ear that had caught his fancy. He had laughed his growly laugh, and tickled her cheeks with his luxuriant beard. He was watching the news, not the newsreader, he had assured her, holding her in his arms. Their granddaughter Amrit had walked into the room just then with a book of sums, and they had hurriedly disentangled.

That winter, the tea parties and card playing were brought to an end. Jaspreet had told her that the Prime Minister had been killed by her Sikh bodyguards. Riots had erupted in the city. Even now as she lay in intensive care, tethered to life by machines, she could feel her heart thrash in her chest at the memory of that season. A group of men had broken into their neighbourhood, hunting down Sikh men. They would've found and killed Kulwanti's beloved Jaspreet, her jaan, had it not been for five-and-a-half year old Amrit. That little khoti had found a unique hiding place for her grandfather. The rioters had gone back after banging on the gate of the old Major, to find out if there was a Sikh hiding somewhere in his house. There was, her jaan Jaspreet was there, but the Major didn't say anything to the men. Major Budhwar, whose spine was bent like the milky gourd he grew in his vegetable garden, proved that evening that hot blood coursed through his veins, not tomato juice. Because of him, and that khoti Amrit, Jaspreet had lived on, only to die years later of a grand heart attack in their four-poster bed.

Her thoughts drifted to Amrit. How quickly she had grown to become a woman. What a little moron—well into her thirties, and still not married. Always scribbling in that notebook of hers, always fighting with that son-of-a-donkey editor of hers, and never meeting nice men to marry. Kulwanti tried to bang her fists against the railings of the hospital bed—her great-grandchildren were not born yet, how could she die without pinching their cheeks and making them howl?

Kulwanti was certain that Amrit was crying softly outside. The khoti. She should go home and get some sleep. She should know that her grandmother was preparing to meet a new friend, for a tea party in eternity. She should know that the only thing that frightened her grandmother was the prospect of meeting this new friend with deep lines on her face, caused by an over-tight oxygen mask.

II

Visitors were not allowed inside the intensive care unit, but the hospital made allowances for the loved ones of the almost dead.

Amrit leaned over her grandmother. How tiny she looked in that bed with its knobs and machines—like a fragile winged creature that had crash-landed in a strange city with flashing lights, beeping monitors, tubes of blood and other fluids. How helplessly tangled in this web of intravenous medicines. Amrit was certain that Kulwanti was anything but dead; she was in a rage, even though she lay under layer upon layer of sedatives and antibiotics. The nerves on her forehead were taut, like electric wires on the verge of sparking before a thunderstorm. They always bulged out of her forehead when she was about to have one of her 'royal sardarni tantrums'; as Amrit's grandfather Jaspreet had lovingly named those fierce bouts of name-calling, teeth-baring (in her mature years, denture-baring), charging-at-the-offender-with-a-pair-of-knitting-needles rages. She was in the midst of a silent tantrum now; Amrit could sense that Kulwanti resented her inability to use her arms, legs and vocal chords to express horror and shame at her current state.

She had probably heard the wailing; Kulwanti had, without a doubt, heard all the sighs and whispers of traumatized flesh and troubled souls inside the hospital. The wailing, drowned out by the hospital's digitized bhajans, had emanated from the part of the hospital cordoned off as 'Emergency'. It had formed a network of sobs that had trickled through the hospital's outpatient departments—ENT, Ophthalmology, Medical Oncology, Pediatrics—vacant now, for it was well past midnight. It had spared the outpatients its incessant pronouncement of death, but had managed to disturb the silence of the waiting room outside the intensive care unit, where Amrit lay slumped on a plastic chair.

'Very big tragedy, ma'am, a child has died...ninety percent burns, ma'am...' a nurse carrying a prescription chart had informed her. 'Whole family is in wedding clothes, ma'am... whole family is crying in wedding clothes,' she had turned around and said, before the darkness of the intensive care unit had consumed her.

Amrit had followed the nurse in. She had wanted to tell Kulwanti about the dead child; she had wanted her grandmother to sit bolt upright on the bed surrounded by its twinkling city of machines; she had wanted her grandmother to beat her chest and howl into the still night of the intensive care, to shake the sick and the dying who lay around her with news of the stiff little body and its loved ones in their rich brocades.

And now, as she sat beside her grandmother, she let her tears fall on Kulwanti's face. 'Wake up,' she whispered. 'A child has died, at a wedding function...I think...the body has burns...wake up...find out what happened...wake up... scold the gods for taking a child...wake up...take the crying mother into your arms...wake up...make arrangements for the body to be bathed...wake up...just wake up.'

III

'No talking in the ICU, ma'am, otherwise we will ask you to leave,' said the nurse.

Kulwanti could hear voices whispering the intensive care unit. Probably that khasma-nu-khani in the white skirt-and-blouse, with coarse and curly hair on her arms that had prickled Kulwanti's own traumatized flesh, whenever she came near enough to gaze at the monitors, or to raise an ill-shaped eyebrow at Kulwanti's vitals beeping away on the screen. Didn't she know that talking wasn't allowed in this section of the hospital, where each laboured breath was a roll number that announced a life tethered to its end?

Someone else was hovering over her—Amrit. So the little khoti had managed to get into the ICU. Kulwanti could feel her granddaughter's fingertips tremble against her own skin. A teardrop fell on her creased forehead and trickled down one side of her face. She tried to move her jaw to speak, but the oxygen mask restricted movement and smothered her words. She was aware that Amrit's face had tilted when that moron of a nurse had spoken. Amrit, with a heart like a jalebi, sweet and messy, that khoti, who even now would weep herself soggy whenever she saw a butterfly ripped apart on the thorny branches of the rose bushes in the garden, was probably crying over the dead child she had been whining about a few moments ago. Wetting her grandmother's face with tears for an anonymous near-and-dear.

Kulwanti wanted to shut her granddaughter up. If she really needed a good cry, she should go wherever it was the dead child lay, and cry over it. Not here. Children died all the time in this city; they suffocated themselves with too much chocolate cake at birthday parties, they drowned in swimming pools, they fell into open sewers. Sometimes one saw their photos in the obituaries section of *The Times of India*—in frilly frocks or baba suits. Photos taken from family albums. Photos that didn't anticipate a grainy version of themselves appearing in the dead-people's pages. And sometimes, there was no picture of the child. There was just something that belonged to the child, like a school bag or a pair of shoes that appeared in the newspaper, on the front page. Kulwanti had seen a picture many years ago, the year the lady Prime Minister was killed—a tiny pair of shoes with pom-poms on the toes, on the footpath adjoining an empty road. The newspaper had given the photo a catchy caption—*A Childhood Lost in a Riot.* Kulwanti had read it out aloud and in perfect English to Jaspreet, who had frowned. No one knew the name of the child whose shoes had appeared in the morning news. But Jaspreet had snuffled loudly, just like Amrit was snuffling now.

Go, cry over the dead, Kulwanti wanted to scream, baring her toothless gums through the oxygen mask. She was alive. Couldn't they hear the monitor beep, and the green line on it ripple and swell in agitation?

Rikhi Book Depot

I

The balconies curved and swelled like wrought-iron wombs on the dirty façade of the buildings. The remnants of an age of elegance, thought Amrit as she peered out of the rickshaw. The buildings looked as though they would crumble in a heap of bricks, cement, shop owners and customers if one leaned against a wall, or thwacked a spider crawling to its more substantial masonry of webs. The paint had peeled off a long time ago, and crusty membranes of plaster often fell onto the pavement. The brickwork stood exposed to a world too modern and too busy to pause and marvel at its durability. Leaky water pipes made the walls drip, and formed islands of mould on their uneven surface.

But the balconies, with their antique filigree that looked like torn lace, stood in defiance of the shabbiness that surrounded them. Amrit looked up and saw a line of towels, underwear and trousers dangling from the railings. This was where they must have once stood, she thought, squinting her eyes and shading them with her hand. This was where the wives and daughters of the traders of Chandni Chowk, fattened by leisure and the prosperity of their merchant menfolk, must have stood, drying their hair in the sunshine, or calling out to the neighbourhood paanwala for their daily fix. She wondered whether the dull stains on the walls were from casual emissions of scarlet paan spittle. She imagined those women with freshly hennaed hair, leaning against the balconies to gossip with one another, or to observe the lalas in the gali below conduct their business of fabric and spice. They must have spat the red juice collecting in their mouths with such abandon, she thought. But could paan stains last for years, surviving the transition from Chandni Chowk, that bazaar dappled with moonlight, to this wretched gali with its crumbling buildings and rickshaws that bumped into one another as they wound their way through piles of garbage, cow dung, and children playing pithu? Probably not. Only the balconies had survived the transition, and remained indifferent to the changes wrought in the women who leaned against the railings as eras came and went—from voluptuous figures draped in rich fabrics to scrawny, overworked hags, picking lice from the matted heads of their children.

The rickshaw bumped into a rehdi full of sweet lime and kinnow, startling Amrit out of her reverie. It nearly overturned the cart before coming to a halt outside Rikhi Book Depot. A few pieces of the fruit fell to the ground and the rehdiwala bent down to pick them up. After he had gathered them, he mumbled, without making eye contact with the rickshawala: 'Madarchod!'

Amrit paid the rickshawala quickly, sensing an imminent scuffle. She crushed her urge to haggle, even though she knew he had overcharged her for the short ride from Chandni Chowk metro station to Nai Sarak. She climbed down from the vehicle and saw that two little boys—rag pickers, or tiny thugs, or both—had attached themselves to the rear of the rickshaw by clinging to its iron bars, and had travelled with her—a fact that was secret to none but her. She squealed, but the boys simply jumped off the rickshaw and walked away, as though all they wanted was a free ride to a street lined with shops that sold textbooks they couldn't read.

Ruffians! Pickpockets! Urchins! This was not the Chandni Chowk of the old capital of Shahjahanabad. And this was definitely not the Chandni Chowk of Bollywood, with its damsels singing on low-lying roofs, its naujawans with a Bullet 500 or a Classic Desert Storm throbbing between their legs, its mirzas reduced to penury, who gurgled on hookahs on street corners all day long.

This was the Chandni Chowk of petty criminals, and Nai Sarak, with its shops that sold books for every possible entrance exam—Medical, Engineering, Law, CA CPT, UPSC—was ideal for them to hone their skills in stealth and speed. There were ample opportunities to crawl into a shop, when a shopkeeper was busy bargaining with students, or sat comatose because of the heat. The ragamuffins could stuff a few books into their underpants and slip out, into the crowded gali, which led to the main road, where they could sell the books at a traffic intersection. But this was mere guesswork.

Amrit was being fanciful; there were other things the boys could have stolen in Chandni Chowk, which would have been more lucrative for selling on the streets. Like the spare parts of cars, motorcycles and trucks.

II

Amrit stood outside Rikhi Book Depot. The woman who sat behind the counter held the receiver of a black Beetel landline against the slack folds of her left cheek. An identical red telephone lay next to the black one. A silver locket with the Sikh emblem—the double-edged sword, surrounded by a chakkar and flanked on either side by two single-edged swords—hung from her chest and rose and fell to the rhythm of her breathing. A framed photograph of a middle-aged sardar hung on the wall behind her, partly covered in cellophane paper. The gigantic garland of plastic flowers that hung from the photograph grazed the woman's head.

Amrit waited by the counter, but when the woman continued to speak in rapid Punjabi into the phone without so much as glancing at her, she moved closer to a bookshelf. The frayed spines of *Paradise Lost*, *Principles and Practices of Banking*, *Frankenstein*, *Utopia*, *Marriage and Divorce Laws*, *The Doctor's Dilemma* lay stacked together, uncategorized by either genre or milieu. A ladder stood at a slant, its uppermost rung grazing a gigantic volume of *Political Thought*. *Silas Marner* lay wedged between *Delhi Development Act, 1957, with Allied Acts, Rules and Regulations*, and *History of Medieval India*. She tried to pull the novel out and immediately caused a minor dust storm on the shelves. Better not to touch anything, she thought, or Milton and Mary Shelley and Sir Thomas More and Shaw and all the very learned people who formulated theories and legitimized radical thought would come crashing down, and who knew if the pages of the books might splinter into a million pieces, damaged as they were by termites and silverfish.

The shelves that drew the most customers were the *Competition Refresher* and the *Kit of Interviews* series. Very little dust had been allowed to settle on these exam guidebooks, which were freshly bound and stacked in neat piles. The prospective examinees who lived within the ramparts of the Red Fort were all aspiring engineers, or doctors, or civil servants. What would that penniless maker of couplets—Ghalib, whose haveli in Gali Qasim Jan had only recently been repaired and turned into a ticketed venue of historical significance—have thought of an entire generation that could learn and recite someone else's thoughts by rote, but couldn't write their own thoughts on a page, let alone make poetry?

Prosaic but ambitious. Amrit was disappointed with the few students in the shop—probably boys and girls from the mohallas and bazaars around Nai Sarak. It would be futile to talk to them. To these young people, born after 1984, the Prime Minister's assassination was just a multiple-choice question—*When was India's third Prime Minister killed? a) 31 October, 1984, b) 2 November, 1984, c) 5 December 1985.*

Did they know, these kids, with their carefully trimmed

stubbles, and fake Dolce & Gabbana logos on their t-shirts, did they know that it was here, in Rikhi Book Depot, that someone had tried to start a fire all those years ago? Did they know that if a matchstick had been lit and thrown on the floor of this bookshop, Nai Sarak, where the streets are lined with paper—textbooks, calendars, wedding cards, visiting cards—would have turned into a heap of ash? The wind would have lifted the ash and scattered the remains of cindered literature across the ramparts of the Red Fort. Ash would have filled the fluted dome of Fatehpuri Masjid. Charred books would have demanded last rites; they would have formed their own memorial of embers, ablaze with the fury of dying unread, impossible to demolish.

Amrit moved slowly towards the counter; if there was anyone who knew why Rikhi Book Depot had not been burnt down that day in 1984, it was the woman with the phone receiver stuck to her ear. Everywhere else, the city had been a steady blaze of homes, shops and sardars. But Nai Sarak had been spared, even though most of the shops here were owned by Sikhs. She wanted to write about this 'lucky episode'. She was certain that her editor at the national daily she worked for would call it that. But this lucky episode could also be the scoop she was looking for, in the series of stories about the 1984 riots that she intended to research and write on. A series her editor had already dismissed as an 'exercise in futility'. He had ticked her off for 'wasting precious working days on stale stories'. He had told her that many reporters, more 'seasoned and skilled' than her, had already written about those few days of rampaging and murder, soon after the Prime Minister was killed by her Sikh bodyguards.

But Amrit wasn't here because she wanted to impress her editor with unknown facts about the riot. She was here because of her Dadaji, who had nearly died that year. She was here because she had finally embarked upon her own investigation of the riots, after years of reporting on inanities. All the stories she had heard from Dadaji, about a barsati that was burned down, about shops that were looted, about men who disappeared, about FIRs that could never be found, had led her to this self-assigned research and reportage that was of no consequence to anyone but herself. She was here because she had promised Dadaji that she would be here, and in every other place that had been besieged by a crowd that wanted blood for blood, many lives for one fallen leader, genocide for assassination.

'Sardar ka bachcha murdabad!' they had shouted, and she could hear them now, as though they stood outside Rikhi Book Depot, pelting it with stones.

III

'The market was closed on that day. As you can see, Amrit puttar, most of the shops here belong to sardar families,' said the woman behind the counter, who had finally put the black Beetel receiver into its groove on the landline. Amrit had hovered near the counter and made relentless eye contact with the woman, hoping that she looked more beseeching and less demanding of attention or service. The woman, Gurleen Sikka, had succumbed to Amrit's persistence and had acknowledged her presence by asking, 'Tenu ki chahida, puttar?' When Amrit had informed her that she was a reporter who wanted to write about Rikhi Book Depot for a national daily, Gurleen had asked her to take a seat. Then she had hollered, 'Jogi, Jogi oye Jogi,' until a boy in dirty brown half-pants and a vest had appeared. Gurleen had ordered a Limca, and flung a few crushed notes at the boy, who had grabbed the money and disappeared. Jogi had reappeared almost immediately, with the Limca, which Gurleen had pushed towards Amrit, while saying, 'Feel comfortable; this is your shop, puttar!'

They now sat facing each other. The photograph of the dead Sikh man loomed over them. 'My chachaji, Rikhi,' said Gurleen, 'who died that day.' She dabbed her eyes with the edges of her chiffon dupatta. 'I was only nineteen, puttar, too young to beat my chest and cry, but I did...I opened my hair...I swung my head round and round...I cried like all the other women in the gali...I...I...Hai Rabba! My young life has seen so much...'

Amrit, who sipped her Limca through a straw while Gurleen spoke, paused, and kept the bottle on the glass counter. She felt ashamed for making an elderly woman cry. The few students in the shop were staring at them now. She should have been gentler and more discreet in her enquiries; the riot was a trauma wedged in the memories of so many Sikhs, she ought to have understood that better than anyone else. Dadaji had wept openly whenever he had spoken of those few days of curfew and the sirens of police vans that had patrolled the city but done nothing to check the rioting.

'We don't have to talk about it…Please don't cry, aunty…I'm sorry…We really don't have to…' Amrit managed to say.

'Then how will you know, how will you newspaper-walas, who only write stories about how many died and how many were injured, how will you ever know that in this story, two men die, but a market is saved,' Gurleen pressed her dupatta to her forehead, which glistened with sweat. The words came out in a rush.

'We know that the shops in Nai Sarak were not burnt down. That's why I'm here, to find out why these shops were looted but not set on fire.' Amrit felt her words quiver when she spoke.

'Nai Sarak did not burn that day, because Rikhi Chacha here…' Gurleen tugged at the plastic flower garland that hung over her head. 'Bec…because Rikhi Chacha here, was killed. He was killed, but the books…these books….and all the other books in Nai Sarak lived…they lived…and if they could speak…they would tell you that Rikhi Chacha was killed so that they could live…so that they could be read by these mushtandas and mushtandis who are preparing for their exams…'

Gurleen spoke with deranged abandon; Amrit allowed her to. Her memories were vivid, urgent, and would not tolerate restraint or interruptions. It was the second or third day after the Prime Minister had been shot. Nai Sarak was run by sardar businessmen—wholesalers of textbooks and calendars who had pulled down the shutters of their shops the moment Delhi was declared under curfew. Rikhi Chacha was not supposed to be in the shop on that day, when the rioters broke into Rikhi Book Depot. But fate had placed him there, at the exact moment when the rioters smashed the lock on the shutter and tumbled into the bookshop.

'He had gone to remove the cash from the big Godrej safe in the shop. We begged him not to go, but he said, "So far, nothing has happened in Chandni Chowk. Let me go. Why should our hard-earned money fall into the hands of goondas?" He kick-started his Bajaj Priya and rode away in the empty street. We...we...ne...ne...ver...saw...w...we...never...saw him again puttar...' Gurleen's words came out in fissured phrases; she dabbed her eyes with her dupatta.

Amrit put her arms around Gurleen, who sobbed into her neck. The few students who were in the shop had gathered around the counter. One of them, a boy in tight jeans and a t-shirt that said *Live Like Singh*, frowned at Amrit.

Gurleen pulled herself away from Amrit and tried to recover her composure. She blew her nose into her dupatta and shooed the students away from the counter.

'Don't just stand in my shop...if all you want to do is stare at me...go...go...read something...we have paid a very high price for these books you are holding in your hands...these books that you are holding and not buying.' She then paused before saying, 'If you want to buy a book, then come to the counter, okay?'

The students drifted away. Gurleen pushed a strand of silver hair behind her ear and said, 'So sorry puttar, I didn't know there were so many tears still left in me...but let me tell you, let me tell you how Rikhi Chacha died, before I am too old and can only weep and not find the words...'

Amrit sat close to Gurleen as she spoke. Rikhi Chacha did not return from the shop, which was a few galis away from where they lived. Gurleen's father was about to set off on his scooter to search for his younger brother when someone arrived at the door. It was Hakim Zahid Raza, who ran a dawakhana in a corner of Nai Sarak. The little shop that sold Unani concoctions for everything from mouth ulcers to paralytic strokes had remained open because the old hakim believed that no rioter could ever enter Chandni Chowk—the ramparts of the Red Fort made it impenetrable. 'Lahori Gate will keep the murderers away,' he had declared, and the relative safety of Chandni Chowk had confirmed his belief in the strength of its architecture. Until that day. Hakim Zahid's son, Aziz, who ran the shop, had made a worrying telephone call. He had seen a group of men in Nai Sarak. They were carrying lathis and car tyres; they were walking towards Rikhi Book Depot. Was there someone inside the shop, Aziz had asked. The shutter had been lifted and was half open.

'Just close the dawakhana and come home,' the old hakim had croaked into the telephone receiver.

But Aziz, like Rikhi Chacha, had not returned.

'Sardar sahib, it would be unwise to ride your scooter into the riot. The boys will come home; all we can do is wait,' Hakim Zahid had said.

Gurleen's body quaked as the memory taunted her.

IV

Amrit stood facing a shelf with *Prakash Yadav's Class Notes* jammed between *Molly Flanders* and *Joseph Andrews.* So this is where Rikhi Chacha must have died, she thought, her body wedged in the space between the bookshelves. Rikhi Book Depot was empty now; it was early evening and the students had left after purchasing compilations of sample papers. Gurleen, exhausted from recalling past horrors, was sipping tea from a flask that Jogi had produced from a wicker basket.

'Don't burn the books!' Was that what Rikhi chacha had said, to those men with their cans of kerosene? Did he plead with them, or did he command them? Amrit would never know. But Aziz, who had seen the partially lifted shutter, and had run to Rikhi Book Depot, had not had the time to run out of the bookshop, it was said. His body had been found inside a steel trunk used for storing second-hand books. Had Rikhi chacha pushed him in? Was he about to jump into the trunk himself, when the men arrived? The events that led to the murders of Aziz and Rikhi chacha would forever be patched together by guesswork, mostly, and only some actual evidence. Rikhi chacha's body lay soaked in blood on a heap of torn books. Pages of literature had been ripped apart for a funeral pyre made of stories and poems.

It was whispered that Rikhi Book Depot did not burn down that day because Rikhi chacha had read passages from his favourite books, to the rioters. The myth had gathered momentum over the years; it hovered like a cloud of words and phrases, uttered by a man who was about to die, around Rikhi Book Depot, around Nai Sarak—the one 'lucky episode' in a history of unfortunate ones.

'Don't burn the books!' Amrit imagined Rikhi Chacha screaming. They must have grabbed him by the head and torn his turban off.

'Why?' they would have asked. 'Tell us why we shouldn't burn the books. Wouldn't you like to lie on a pyre of books?'

Maybe the rioters were about to pour petrol on the pile of books, when Rikhi chacha had managed to pull one out. His fingers may have trembled like leaves in a storm, when he opened a page and began to read:

'The night was very silent, and the moon was going down,
And the winds of dawn were chilling all the sea.'

Amrit imagined him reading Kipling, and Hardy, and Mulk Raj Anand. Did he read Gandhi? Or Rousseau? Did he read from the *Principles of Accounting*? Or *Essays in East West Philosophy?* They had threatened to set the shop on fire and he had made their ammunition—the books—speak to them, at least for a few moments. He had grasped wildly at the books and read snatches of sentences from random pages: 'Panchi tried to imagine what the girl, Gauri, was like: Was she fair or was she dark?' Or maybe, this: 'When Farmer Oak smiled, the corners of his mouth spread till they were within an unimportant distance of his ears, his eyes were reduced to chinks…'

The impromptu performance must have been a short recess during the looting of Rikhi Book Depot. Amrit could almost hear the rioters consult each other, as they stood around Rikhi chacha, watching him read, 'Ma Saraswati… Should we burn Ma Saraswati?'

But Rikhi chacha, they had killed him as he had read, slitting his throat with, was it a kirpan? He had fallen on the pile of books; the blood spurting out of the gash on his neck had turned the yellowing pages of some of the books a bright red.

'Are there any surviving eye-witnesses of this account… someone from a neighbouring shop? Amrit asked a little officiously, feeling foolish almost immediately.

Gurleen looked at her as though she would throw the half-empty glass of tea at her. 'You don't believe me, puttar? You don't believe that Rikhi chacha, whose shop you are standing in, read from these books so that the goondas, who had never held a book in their hands, would know…they would understand…that books are vidya, books are gyan…

burning a book is a greater sin than burning a Sikh man... you don't believe that Rikhi chacha saved all the books of Nai Sarak, puttar?'

'Aunty...please don't misunderstand...this story is for the newspaper...I need an eyewitness...a source...'

'Come with me, puttar.' Gurleen pushed herself away from the counter and got up. She squeezed herself in the space between the shelves, where Amrit stood. She produced a bunch of keys from the layers of her salwar-kameez. She picked one from the jumble and opened a small wooden cabinet that stood by a bookshelf.

'Let me show you some books. Their pages are red—the colour has faded over the years, but they are the only source, the only witnesses...' Gurleen's voice was steady and cold.

Amrit wondered if her editor would want to see the blood-stained books. 'How can we be sure if this is the blood of Rikhi of Rikhi Book Depot?' Amrit was certain he would ask. How can we be sure of anything, really?

Satnam Taxi Service

I

The radio on Satnam Pal Singh's shiny new phone played his favourite song. 'Bullah ki jaana main kaun,' sang the pop-Sufi singer on 98.3 FM, his voice rising to a crescendo as he crooned a dilemma first uttered by that metaphysical Punjabi, Bulleh Shah. Satnam contemplated the words of the song.

'I know not who I am,' thought Satnam, 'like Bullah, I too know not who I am.'

The phone lay on the colossal heap of undulating flesh that was Satnam's stomach, exposed to the world after a heavy lunch of tadke-wali-daal, aloo-gobhi, parathas, and raw onions. He had unbuttoned his shirt and collapsed on a stringy manji, in a stupor heightened by the afternoon heat. Having fiddled with his phone and stumbled upon the song just as he was about to tune into another frequency, Satnam had allowed himself a lazy wallow in the pool of profound thoughts the lyrics had created for him.

Satnam wasn't given to deep contemplation; he was a

businessman who ran a fairly successful taxi rental service in the bustling interiors of South Delhi. He was proud that his taxi stand, with its fleet of black-and-yellow cars, as well as the more expensive vehicles like the dial-a Toyota Innova and Mercedes Benz had survived the economic whiplash brought about by the newer radio cab services, with their online booking facilities and nationwide networks of taxis of all shapes and sizes.

He would twirl his luxurious moustache, run his fingers through the silken grey mane of his beard, and feel the curvature of his belly to draw the attention of prospective customers to his obvious prosperity. He would then join his hands reverentially and whisper a brief prayer of thanks to Babaji—Guru Nanak, the source of his benedictions. Those who had witnessed these sudden bursts of piety had assumed that Satnam was praying to one of the taxis parked at the stand. He would then attend to calls—his mobile phone rang incessantly during the summer months—and bargain loudly with customers, arbitrarily hiking up the fares with his standard excuse: 'Meter is old, fuel too much costing. I poor man, I live on grace of Babaji. Pliz pay...' This was usually followed by an amount he deemed fit—if the customer was well-off or foreign, he would fleece them with a disarming sweetness.

Satnam's father, Sukhwinder, who was now 'none more', had also worked in a taxi stand near the airport. Sukhwinder too, had been prone to overcharging foreign tourists. He had died when his son was still too young to understand the trickeries of swindling exhausted travellers who lay slumped in the back seat of his Amby. But Satnam's mother, Nirmal Kaur, had raised him to become the shrewd 'bijji-ness-man' he was, commandeering gleaming taxis that would have astonished his father.

The song (and the post-lunch lull) put him in a philosophical mood. He wondered about the state of his existence, and the lyrics prodded him to consider his insignificance. 'I am neither Arab, nor am I from Lahore; I am neither Hindu, nor Turkish, nor am I from Peshawar,' sang the voice on the radio, in Punjabi. Satnam nodded his turbaned head, agreeing with the poet's sentiment. He was but a taxi-driver, or, from a deeper perspective that matched his present state-of-mind, a Sikh who had been allowed to grow up and make a living, marry a decent-looking sardarni from Faridkot, 'reproduce plumpy babies' (as he said to his foreign clients), and become the owner of a fleet of taxis—all by the grace of Babaji and the good karma his ancestors had accumulated over generations. He was but a tiny speck of dust, a grain of jowar or bajra being sifted in a wicker sieve—his similes grew more fanciful as the song progressed—whose life would have been cut, like a tender stalk of sugarcane hacked before its time, had it not been for the timely protection he had received from celestial sources.

It was his mother's quick thinking and nimble-footedness that had kept him alive, he reminded himself. She had not collapsed when rioters had walked into their residential colony and flung car tyres around all the necks of the menfolk, including Sukhwinder. She had not paused to retch in the open drains when the smell of burning flesh and hair had reached her as she ran with five-year-old Satnam clinging to her like a terrified goat. She had run across streets scattered with arms and legs, and had paused only to quench their thirst with their own urine. Satnam had howled when she had forced the yellow liquid down his gullet, but she had squeezed his nostrils shut and made him drink it. She had then lifted the sobbing boy in her arms and trudged across a city littered with the dead and inhabited by the inconsolable, to the temporary relief of a camp, set up hurriedly in safer areas for those who managed to stumble in.

Satnam almost threw up at the memory but the phone rang, interrupting the song and lessening the shock of the past with the immediacy of business.

'Who's calling?' he wondered as he answered the phone.

He heard Mallika Khanna's polite and distant 'Hello? Sardarji?' as the phone flashed yet another incoming call. South Delhi was up after an afternoon siesta, and his services were very much in demand. There was no time to indulge memories, and anyway, *Time is Money*, announced the cardboard signage he had pasted on the electric pole outside his taxi stand.

II

The day broke in warm orange tones, but rapidly brightened to an incandescent lemon that hurt the eyes. Mallika Khanna decided not to go to work. The temperature inside her air-conditioned room was a comfortable twenty-one degrees Celsius, while outside, the ripe summer tincture of the morning suggested a sharp rise to forty degrees. She pulled the light Jaipuri quilt up to her chin and decided to huddle in its warmth for a few moments before hollering for a cup of tea. She would take it easy. She would have breakfast in bed—a strong cup of cardamom-clove-ginger tea, fried eggs (sunny side up, non-leaky yolks), two slices of wholegrain bread, toasted, buttered and layered with mint chutney.

She wondered if she should call her boss and invent an excuse for taking the day off. She could cough into the phone and feign an illness, but that would be too obvious. She could say that an aunt was arriving in Delhi after a long transatlantic flight, and she had to be at the airport to receive her. She could claim that Mr Cocoa, her cocker spaniel, needed to have his nails clipped. Or, she could simply not bother to call him. She was convinced he wouldn't notice her absence—he barely noticed when she was there, working with such efficiency, meeting every deadline so he could step out for a boozy lunch with his gang of fawning underlings.

Mallika flung the blanket aside and got out of bed. She wasn't going to waste the day, thinking toxic thoughts or imagining conspiracy theories. She stretched languorously, then decided to touch her toes to warm-up, and speed-up her sluggish blood circulation. Maybe she should step outside and roll out her yoga mat on the lawn. A few Surya Namaskaras would make her sweat away the poison of dislike and fill her with fellow feelings towards man and beast, *and* her boss.

Her tea arrived in a telepathic gesture of empathy—she was about to poke her head out of the room and call for it, but Jagannath, the family cook, knew she was up. She smiled at him groggily as he carefully unfolded a tea table, balanced it on the bed and placed the tea on it—without making a sound or splashing a drop.

Mallika promptly crept back into her blanket the moment he left the room. She would sip her tea and check her email, just to make sure there were no immediate briefs on her job list.

Her inbox was full. She was scheduled to make a presentation at three in the afternoon to the cream biscuit company that had recently been added to the firm's roster of clients. Her ideas for a thirty-second television commercial (her boss had nearly sabotaged her campaign) were up for discussion today. She brightened at the thought of shooting the commercial with a celebrity—a Bollywood star, or even a cricket player? Her boss had insisted that the commercial needed a song, and had even scribbled his own ditty—in a narcotics-whisky stupor—which he had handed her on a grubby scrap of paper.

When you need a break, why eat cake?
When life is a puzzle and the pieces don't fit,
Have an Innocent Child Cream Biscuit. (Repeat).

Voice Over: Innocent Child Cream-filled Biscuits. Available in Chocolate, Vanilla and Strawberry flavours.

She had nodded politely when he had recited it to her, raising her eyebrows and looking delighted when he had broken into song, mid-sentence. She had then added the song to the scripts that she had mailed him, but not to the final draft—the one she would present today, if she decided to go.

There were other emails. An unimaginative resignation letter, reeking servility: *I humbly thank everyone for the opportunity to work, learn and grow here*—grow into what, a spineless creature with brains the size of a biscuit crumb? There was an invitation to an office party, organized by one of the cock-sucking toadies, 'in honour of BOSS's new campaign for Smooth & Easy shaving cream. Come with your spouse, or your spice!!' She had neither, so she would probably skip.

She wondered what the old school—creative directors who wore three-piece-suits or silk saris to work, in an era often described as advertising's heyday, when copywriters knew their punctuation marks—would think of the crowd that filled an agency these days. The ones who had arrived from Bhatinda, or Begusarai, and had immediately discarded their kurta-pyjamas to struggle into slim-fit jeans. The ones who had tasted sudden success and had turned into celebrities overnight, wearing their oversized sunglasses to work and sipping their expensive Scotch as they discussed their next thirty-second TV spot to be directed by a hot new director for a price that could build a school, or feed an entire city. She wondered how the grand old copywriters and art directors would feel, when they saw an upstart creative director discussing a campaign idea with some sweet young thing, the distance between his legs increasing with every tremulous breath she took, in that rarefied space called a glass cabin.

Toxic thoughts. And deeply bigoted ones too—she had no business judging people from the dusty bowels of the motherland. She was just being a South Delhi bitch, an *idle* South Delhi bitch, the kind she despised more than any creative director from Begusarai. She would call Satnam for a cab, and get her ample rump to work. She would be marked 'half-day present' but she would be on time for her presentation.

III

'Pleease send taxi, Sardarji, office jana hai,' Satnam mimicked Mallika Khanna with an ease that made Dalbir, one of the younger cab drivers who worked at the stand for a daily wage, laugh. They were accustomed to the random order in which the days of these people unfolded. Satnam had received calls at four in the morning, requesting a cab that would take the caller to a motel on the other side of town—for an early breakfast meeting with a client, no less. A harami with a hard-on, Satnam had thought, as he had woken up one of his boys. A woman had once called him, in the throes of labour pain, barely able to utter the words, 'Hospital...baby coming!' She was alone at home; her husband was travelling for 'bijjniss–shijniss', her parents lived in another city, and there was no one else she could have called. In a country full of second cousins, grandaunts, nieces and nephews, she had made it to the hospital alone for her first delivery. And Satnam, who had driven like a maniac, although he had been careful enough to circumvent potholes, had been the first to receive the news of the birth.

'A plumpy girl is come, by Babaji's grace,' he had announced to his employees.

He wondered what kind of job this Mallika Khanna had, and if she was any good at it. To arrive at work at two in the afternoon was an absolute shame. Wasn't she grateful to whichever god she prayed to, for a job that paid her so well, for her parents who allowed her to wake up so late in the day, for the food that was cooked for her by somebody else?'

'A silly-billy girl,' he thought, not wanting to use harder words for his spoilt, young but regular customer.

He wondered how old she was—definitely older than his mother had been when she had first started working.

They had been herded into a bus and sent back from the relief camps to Trilokpuri—their home before the riot had turned it into a neighbourhood of the dead. He remembered how the empty houses had stared at the returning residents—their broken window panes dark and hollow, like eyes that had cried a river and were now forever dry. The few packets of dal, rice and flour they had received as token nourishment, from a government that had lost its patience with all the wailing and chest-beating that had accompanied the riot, were crawling with insects and rat droppings.

Satnam's mother had taken up a job in a local municipal school, as an ayah for the primary classes. Nirmal Kaur had scrubbed the floors and cleaned the backsides of the children. She had made tea and pakodas in the school canteen. She had woken up at four every morning, to bathe, recite the Japji Sahib, and cook for Satnam before leaving for work by the six-o-clock bus. Later, she had put him in the same school, for an education that relied heavily on books, uniforms and even rations of food donated by the teachers.

Mallika Khanna was a fat blotch on the face of all working women who had sacrificed their youth, their beauty, their sleep, to cook hot chapattis for their children at home, Satnam thought angrily. But then, there was another incoming call that flashed its urgency on his phone.

IV

He would do her, and do her, and do her. In her father's shop. Between the sacks of basmati, flour, and sugar. In the tiny store room behind the shop, leaning against a rickety wooden shelf stacked with tea, cooking oil, papad, and aloo bhujiya.

He would smear cinnamon powder between her thighs and lick it off. He would massage her back. He would drop a green chilli between her parted lips and bite it off, making them both quiver with its heat.

Saurabh Goel had recently been maddened by the sight of Charu, who worked alongside her father in a shop in Khari Baoli, which sold fresh spices and other supplies. Saurabh had found himself navigating the bylanes of the older parts of the city as he collected material for a history project. In his first year at Delhi University, Saurabh had arrived in Old Delhi with a notebook and several sharpened pencils, to make notes and sketches of the mosques, minarets and old havelis that had survived the onslaughts of modernity.

Saurabh had taken the metro to reach Chandni Chowk and had ambled through the market's many bylanes—Dariba Kalan, glimmering in the sun with old gold and kundan jewellery; Nai Sarak, lined with textbooks and compilations of sample question papers; Chawri Bazar, where utensils formed towers of copper and brasss—to finally reach Khari Baoli. The bazar's miniature mountains of spices ran adjacent to Fatehpuri Masjid, which Saurabh was eager to sketch. And it was on his search for the best angle that he first saw her.

She was perched on a sack of rice, in a mung-dal-yellow kurta and tight white churidar. Her silver hoops, carved and painted in the sharp blue, green and yellow of meenakari filigree, had tinkled in delight (he thought), when he had lingered with unnecessary interest over a mound of peppercorns. And when their eyes met, he felt his own unbearable excitement reflected in hers. Her father's ample figure had loomed large over this brief first encounter, but he had managed to convey essential details to her—his name, address and telephone number—written neatly on a page he tore from his notebook.

After a few days of waiting, during which he swung from impatience to anxiety to despair, Charu called. One phone call led to another; each conversation was longer, bolder, riper in intent than the previous. They decided to meet.

Charu would take the metro to his part of town. He would

get back early from college, and hire a black-and-yellow. The cab would take them everywhere—to the multiplexes and food courts, to public parks with their dense foliage, to Connaught Place, where they would sit in the shadows of the pillared corridors and drink flavoured milk. He would take her back to Khari Baoli at dusk, and they would then sneak into her father's shop to finally make love (this was left unsaid, as it depended heavily on whether Charu could get hold of the shop keys that dangled from a hook in her father's room). The cab would be parked outside, waiting for Saurabh to lose his virginity, and to assist in a premature exit in case they were caught.

Saurabh could feel the eagerness building up in his pants as he called Satnam and asked for a cab for half a day, in a voice thick with anticipation. This was a day of great importance; he was going to do it (finally), but not with some daft girl from college, in her jeans and t-shirt, reeking of cigarettes and stale perfume. He was going to do it with a curvy poster-girl of spice, whose breath was nutmeg, whose sweat was cinnamon. And this wasn't going to be a horny afternoon in the life of an undergraduate, it was going to be, his first experiment in anthropological chemistry.

V

Satnam was disgusted. Saurabh sounded like he was up to no good. He had called the taxi stand only once before this, but then, he had wanted a cab to get to college. Today, he sounded vague about where he wanted to go, and worse, he was *very vague* about who would pay for hiring the cab. Previously, his father had settled the bill, but now, Satnam was sure his father wasn't even aware that his son had called him.

Bewakoof mushtandas and mushtandis, he thought. Didn't these young people know how hard their parents, and grandparents had worked so that these silly-billys could call for a taxi whenever they wanted, and waste the peaceful days that Babaji had been kind enough to give them.

He considered not sending the taxis to either of them. Let Mallika Khanna take an auto-rickshaw to office. Let Saurabh Goel walk to wherever he wanted to go. At his age, Satnam would walk for miles to fill up buckets of water at a municipality water tanker that arrived once a week, and parked at arbitrary distances from his home in the Widow's Colony.

He was about to call back and say, 'Sorry-ji, all taxis bijjy,' even though the businessman in him was startled by his empty idealism, when the phone rang. This time, it was his mother. A journalist had arrived in the colony and wanted to speak to its residents. She wanted to make notes about what it was like to run half-way across the city to escape a group of rioters, to grow up without a father (or any male relative), to live off filthy government rations. Nirmal Kaur sounded tired. Could he get home a bit early, and get rid of the journalist? She looked as though she would be happy with a few details of blood and gore.

VI

Nirmal Kaur was on the verge of being impolite to the reporter who sat opposite her, on the cracked floor of her home. She was prepared to talk about the riot, and how she escaped the men who had walked into Block 32, Trilokpuri, all those years ago. She was willing to tell this journalist, Amrit, a juicy story, if that was why she was here, with her open notebook and expressions of deep concern.

But Amrit had not said much. Was she afraid to ask too many questions? Would she be embarrassed if Nirmal Kaur broke down? But Nirmal Kaur's tears had dried up a long time ago...Amrit should speak...she should ask...

'So sad,' was all Amrit was able to mumble, when Nirmal Kaur mentioned that all the menfolk in her family had been murdered in the riot, except her son, Satnam, who was now a successful 'taxi-man' and would soon be home. 'Oh-ho, what a tragedy,' Amrit exclaimed with a sweetness that reminded Nirmal Kaur of overripe fruit on the brink of rot. 'Really? How awful,' she whispered, raising her carefully shaped eyebrows as Nirmal Kaur described the morning of November 1, 1984, when her sixteen-year-old brother-in-law was butchered before the entire family.

Nirmal Kaur wondered if she should send Amrit next door, to her friend Gyani's house. Gyani was older than Nirmal, and had a flair for melodrama. She would probably tell her story with all the graphic details the reporter was looking for. Or Amrit could simply take a walk through the colony and knock on random doors. There was a reason why this settlement of ramshackle buildings, slouching over open sewers and grassless patches of land that had been turned into communal garbage dumps, was called the Widow's Colony. It was meant to be a temporary residence. Tiny apartments had been doled out by the government, to families whose men had been wrenched from them during the riot. But women like Nirmal Kaur, who had moved here once the violence had subsided, had stayed on to rebuild their lives, and raised a generation of children that was fatherless, brotherless, grand-uncleless.

Every family that lived in the Widow's Colony had its own unique tragedy that inhabited the cramped spaces of the apartments, settling like a layer of dust on photographs of the deceased crowding the walls of these homes. Amrit would find enough material here to fill the pages of her notebook. Nirmal Kaur wondered why the country's most popular newspaper had sent *such* an unknown reporter to cover *such* a complex story, although Amrit had tried to convince her that she was a well-known 'features writer' and 'oh, editor too!' Maybe the story was an old one, and had been told often, so the newspaper-walas had sent their most idle journalist to the Widow's Colony.

A reporter's job was far more complicated than making notes and nodding politely, she mused now, as Amrit fidgeted with her notebook. She wondered how long it would take for Satnam to get home. She was weary of retelling the events of a few days in 1984, when the endless summer had given way to a stillborn winter.

VII

'All taxi bijjy, you take Metro, okay,' Satnam had managed to blurt into the phone, when Saurabh had bleated repeatedly for a cab. He had decided not to waste fuel on a tryst into the unknown, indulging the whim of a young mushtanda whose limbs were supple enough to carry him to Old Delhi, if he chose to use them. He had, however, dispatched a black-and-yellow to Mallika Khanna, and had decided to lecture her sometime soon, on the merits of rising with the morning sun and getting to work punctually.

He wondered now, as he drove back home in one of his own taxis, who this journalist was, and what it was that she wanted. He muttered various prayers to the guru on the dashboard, begging for the reporter to leave quickly, without upsetting Nirmal Kaur with senseless questioning. She had been forced to repeat the details of the riot a million times before, and each time, the retelling had left her with a deeper sense of bereavement. A new detail, lodged in memory, would jab her with the intensity of its trauma, and she would find herself talking about the smell of burning hair, or a familiar head, cracked open with a lathi, or bodies left to rot in Trilokpuri's gutters. A fresh drizzle of tears would then threaten to break the dignified reserve she had cultivated over the years, whenever she spoke to the press.

Satnam decided to send the journalist back to her office as quickly as possible, especially if he found that his mother's eyes were red and swollen. He would advise her to do her homework on the massacre—spend time in libraries where all the news reports had been archived, rather than hounding the survivors for information that would resurrect murdered loved ones. He would tell her to take her silly-billy questions elsewhere, preferably to the politicians who had allowed all the Sikhs in Trilokpuri to be killed within a span of three days. But if his gentle attempt to wean her away from discussing the riot did not work, he would simply put her in his cab, and drive her to wherever she worked. And—the bijji-ness-man in him smirked—he would charge her for the ride.

Myself, Sub-Inspector

Myself Balwant Maan, father of Kuldeep Maan and Kaushik Maan. Myself owning two buffaloes, one tractor and one wheat field that is being sometimes fertile, sometimes not, like my wife Manjula. She is being fertile eight years after Kuldeep is born; she is giving me Kaushik, and stopping being fertile after that. Her thighs are drying up, her juices are souring like old milk, but I am still having enough blood in my lund to please the girls of Rohtak, Jhajjar and Sonipat. Even now, I am telling you, even now at sixty-seven, I am getting standing salute every morning from the officer between my legs. But I am not going to be talking and talking about girls—myself old man, grandfathering five grandchildren.

Myself simpleton, myself born to be a farmer, to be tilling the land and milking the buffalos from sun rising to sun setting, like my father and his father. Myself a son of this brown earth. This brown earth is always caring for me like a mother—growing my food and letting me play on her lap under the cool shade of a peepul tree. But the flashing-back thoughts of one season, when this brown earth is becoming red with the blood of innocent chutiyas, is keeping me awake in the night, tossing and tossing in my charpoy, staring and staring at the stars in the black sky, begging whichever devta or shaitan is passing over my charpoy in the darkness to please be bringing me sleep, or death.

Myself not having milk and honey in my veins, or the touch-me-not sensitive soul of a poet—always singing songs on a bullock cart or staring at the full moon like a workless harami—but that one flashing-back thought makes me howl in the night like a kutta.

That thought is troubling and troubling me now, because a few days before, I am having a visitor. She is coming to this village from where I am telling this story, sitting on my charpoy. She is saying she is a journalist. Some Amarpreet or Amrit or something like that. She is holding a notebook close to her mammays. She is saying to me that she is wanting to be talking about that season.

I am talking to her mammays only. I am saying to them, 'What is there to be talking about madamji, everything is happening more than thirty years ago.'

She is covering her mammays with her dupatta and saying that she is wanting to be writing a truthful story about that season.

I am laughing. She is making a face at my teeth that are staining with the red juice of paan. I am asking her mammays if she is thirsty and if she is liking a cold glass of lassi.

She is showing me a bottle of mineral water that is sitting on her chut. She is saying, 'No thank you,' and her voice is soft.

So I am shouting 'Manjula…Manjula!' and that old randi is appearing. I am telling her to be getting one cold glass of lassi for me. I am seeing that through her pallu she is seeing the Dilli girl. I am giving her my bad police afsar look, and she is going running into the kitchen. She is coming back with my lassi, putting it on a stool in front of my charpoy and going running into the kitchen again.

'Tell me, Mister Maan, weren't you the sub-inspector in charge of Kalyanpuri Police Station, in nineteen eighty-four?'

'Yes madamji, I am being sub-inspector,' I am telling her mammays as I am dipping my mouth in the lassi. Lassi is dripping from my moustaches. She is giggling. Her mammays are shaking, like ripe babugoshas that I am wanting to be biting.

'Then tell me,' she is saying, taking out a ball-point pen from her bag and opening her notebook. Her mammays are pressing each other. 'Tell me Mister Maan, where were you on the first of November, all those years ago, when so many Sikhs were killed in your area?'

'Where am I being…where am I being…arre madamji I am being in the police station,' I am saying to her. Where is she thinking I am being? Locked up with some randi on GB Road?

'No…No…I mean…what did you do when the rioters broke into homes in Trilokpuri, which was also within your jurisdiction…Was it not?' she is asking me.

She is using words that are being big and fat. 'I am doing

my duty on that day madamji...Like I am doing my duty every day.'

Myself not being lieful to her, like a little chut who is being told by his teacher to only be speaking truthful things. But myself being clever harami; myself not telling her that myself making very big mistake—going to Dilli, forty years ago, to become a police afsar. Leaving this district, only a little village back then, very big mistake. Myself having good body with bulging muscles and stomach flat like wheat fields. Myself practising kushti every day in the local akhada, fighting the pehalwans of the neighbourhood. Every day, I am practising kushti, eating badaam and drinking buffalo milk. My body is growing stronger and stronger, and I am knowing that I can be helping the police force by beating up all the madarchods this country is producing—goondas, mawalis, hooligans, loiterers—and putting all these sala kuttas in jail. I can be cracking open their empty bhejas like I am cracking open a mungphali. I can be using my biceps for the nation's service, I am thinking. I am fighting with my father to let me go to Dilli.

Myself not telling her all this; myself not telling her what my father, the late Madan Maan is telling me forty years ago.

'Stay here and till the land. Serve the country by feeding its hungry haramzadas,' my father is telling me. I am still hearing his voice booming in my head. 'Stay here,' he is saying, over and over again, but I am packing my steel trunk. 'It is bad there. Either they will kill you, or they will turn you into a filthy madarchod, just like they are,' he is shouting, his voice is cracking like dry earth, but I am grabbing new-born Kuldeep in my arms and pushing Manjula—sobbing like a homeless randi—out of the door. I am leaving for Dilli with my small family, without looking back, without waving tata to my father, without touching the feet of my toothless mother, sitting on the charpoy in the courtyard of our house, holding her rosary and muttering a prayer for me to be turning back. But I am taking a fistful of this brown earth and tying it in a potli before I am leaving. I am belonging to this earth and I am someday returning to this earth, I am telling myself, as I am climbing into the bullock cart that is to be taking us to Dilli.

Myself and Manjula and little Kuldeep are spending the first night in Dilli on the footpath. She is opening her blouse to feed the hungry chutiya, I am standing over them to be making sure no one is looking at them. I am telling her, after Kuldeep is burping and sleeping in her arms, that I am going to buy some food for us. She is saying, 'Don't be leaving us alone.' I am thinking that the jowar rotis and the lassi we are taking with us when we are leaving home are getting over on the way to Dilli, how can I be letting my family starve on the footpath? I am thinking, like a bloodless haramzada, that maybe we should be going back to the village, maybe we will all die on the cruel footpath of Dilli.

By myself and my little family are surviving. A chaiwala is taking us in, and for the first few months in Dilli, I am making chai in his shop for the office-going bhenchods in pants and ties, and Manjula is making bread pakodas, bending over a karhai full of hot oil from morning till evening. I am serving tea; she is washing dishes. I am wiping the tables after the overfed kuttas have licked their plates; she is sweeping the floor. But the old chaiwala is being goodly to us—he is giving us a room to live in and is keeping his hands off my Manjula.

Myself and Manjula and Kuldeep are going on like this (Kuldeep is mostly sleeping and burping through our troubling times) till I am getting a job in the Kalyanpuri Police Station. I am going there, once, twice and three-four times more, but the afsars there are laughing at me and sending me back. I am touching my nose to the ground and doing push-ups, fifty-hundred times, but they are simply drinking their chai and laughing at me. I am show-offing my muscles by holding a bicycle up in the air, but they are laughing. 'Put that down, bhenchod,' they are shouting, 'or spend the night in the lock-up with your favourite randis.'

Myself getting tired of being pleasing to them, but the chaiwala, Narayan sir, is saying to me, 'If your muscles are not impressing them, then try and use your brain.'

But myself simpleton. Myself using my brain like a stingy old seth—in small amounts because I am fearing it will be running out too quickly. But the next time I am at the Kalyanpuri Police Station, I am watching the hawaldars, the sub-inspectors and even the big afsars in their tight pants and shiny shoes. They are looking relaxed and happy only when they are drinking chai. A boy is bringing them chai every afternoon at three pm, in small glasses. They are making noise like kuttas who are seeing a bitch in heat when they are sipping the hot chai.

So myself deciding to make them my special chai, with ginger that I am crushing with my fist. And it is working—I don't know if it is my brain or Narayan sir's advice—but it is working. The police afsars are liking my chai very much. They are saying, 'Wah! This tea is kadak, like a salute.' They are laughing.

'Who has made this damdaar chai?' they are asking. I am appearing before them, joining my hands humbly and smiling softly, at all times looking at my feet, when they are saying, 'You can join tomorrow. But only as an assistant peon.'

Myself telling you, myself finding it difficult to describe my happiness. Myself leaving the service of Narayan sir with a heavy heart. He is hugging me and saying, 'When muscles are not working, use your brains. It is the mostest strongest muscle.'

Myself joining the Kalyanpuri Police Station as Assistant Peon. Myself working very hard, making special chai for afsars when they are coming back to the station after a raid. I am cleaning the desks of all the afsars, arranging the files and putting a fresh glass of water on each table. Sometimes, a friendly afsar is offering me a cigarette—a Charminar Special—for my hard work. And sometimes, I am sharing a pack of bidis with the kaminas in the lock-up. I am feeling badly for them. They are not performing big crimes, like murdering a rich seth, or robbing a bank, or raping a dumb randi. They are small chutiyas who are like me in many ways. They too are leaving their village for the big city. They too are dreaming big dreams. But they are coming here and joining local thieves, or they are selling drugs to school boys to be making money quickly, and they are getting handcuffed by the police. They are not having the good sense, like myself, to be working hard. They are not having people like Narayan sir in their lives, to be giving them goodly advice.

Myself soon getting promotion and becoming peon. And then, by the blessings of that son of the wind, Bajrang Bali, I am getting a chance to show off my muscle strength. A fight is breaking out in one of the lock-ups and I am controlling it by beating up both the criminals. I am going into the lock-up and throwing myself between the two of them. I am separating them; I am kicking their tattes and making them howl. The sub-inspector, who is watching me, is being impressed. He is telling me that if I am really wanting to become a police afsar, I will be having to be taking an exam. I am telling him that I am Senior Secondary borderline pass. He is telling me about the special exam to be joining the police. I will be having to be studying and jogging, in the heat and cold and maybe in the rain, to be passing the theory paper and the physical test.

Myself working in the police station during the day, and studying during the night, after Manjula is serving me dinner and Kuldeep is playing on my lap. I am studying till the dark sky is becoming lighter, like chai with extra milk in it. Then I am jogging on Dilli's footpaths—jumping over open sewers and the bodies of the homeless kaminas who are sleeping like the pavement is their bedroom.

Myself becoming a constable, and am being given a uniform.

Myself catching thieves like the sub-inspector is catching flies all day long, sitting on his chair with his feet on the desk. I am catching them, beating them, and throwing them in the lock-up. I am walking into the parks in the neighbourhood and blowing my whistle, frightening groups of idle bhenchods playing flash and rummy. I am slapping the bottom-pinching and mother-sister teasing men of this city till they are collapsing.

Myself becoming assistant sub-inspector within a few years, and because the sub-inspector is doing nothing but drinking tea, cracking his knuckles and once-in-a-while taking out his belt and hitting a poor bhenchod, I am soon becoming sub-inspector.

Myself enjoying life as an afsar—sipping tea, growing a moustache and killing the mosquitoes in the station, while my constables are bringing me the local goondas. This routine is going on for a few months, but nothing good is lasting for a long time. One day, when I am sitting on my chair and am about to be biting into a motichoor ladoo, the transistor lying on my desk is suddenly crackling with news. It is not being the time for the hourly news, it is being the time for our most favourite programme, *Binaca Geetmala* and the song that is playing, 'Bindiya chamkegi', is being stopped by the serious voice of the Vividh Bharti news reader. The Prime Minister is being shot. She is in hospital. Doctors are trying to be removing bullets from her chest.

Myself thinking, how come the bullets are reaching the Prime Minister's chest if she is wearing a bullet-proof vest?

'She is not wearing the vest,' a constable is whispering, as though he is reading my mind.

'She is walking in her garden and her Sikh bodyguards are shooting her,' someone else is saying.

'SHHH!' The head constable, Sai, is telling. 'Listen to the news. Are you All India Radio?'

We are gathering around the radio set, adjusting and readjusting its antenna so that the crackling is becoming less and the voice that is reading the news is becoming clear. The Prime Minister is being declared dead. There is going to be an acting Prime Minister. The dead Prime Minister's son, who is knowing how to fly a plane but is not knowing how to run a country, is being made the new Prime Minister. The police station is growing silent. It is only being a few hours since the Prime Minister is being shot dead, but already there is being violence in the city. The Sikh President's car is being hit with stones. Riot makers are walking on the road, looking for Sikh men to kill.

Myself getting worried. Kalyanpuri is being full of Sikh ironsmiths. And nearby, Trilokpuri, is also being full of Sikh shop owners and small traders. I am thinking, these are my areas. The time is now coming for me to be protecting the Sikhs here. I am thinking, this is not the time to be sitting on my chair like a harami statue; this is the time to be covering the area with constables, this is the time to be throwing myself at the riot makers and stopping them.

The next day, I am planning a counter-attack strategy with my constables. I am giving orders. Sai is standing next to me. Our strongest constables are standing in a circle around us. These are the men who will be covering Kalyanpuri and Trilokpuri. Already, the police control room wireless is bringing bad news—riot makers are burning buses and making bonfires of Sikh men. They are roaming the streets like mad kuttas. We must be acting quickly. I am dispatching my constables and about to be leaving the station myself, when the phone on my desk is ringing.

'Hello?' I am saying.

'Hello Balwant?' the voice is saying. It is the Station House Officer. My body is automatically becoming straight like an arrow and standing at attention when hearing his voice.

'Good morning sir,' I am saying into the black receiver of the phone.

'Haan, morning. Now listen Balwant, orders from above. Don't do anything right now. You understand?'

'Sir...but sir...the situation outside is becoming bad. It is in the news...' I am managing to say.

'It is under control. Just follow the orders and save your gaand. Okay?' He is barking at me before the line is going dead.

Myself is shaking all over. Myself is telling Sai to call the boys back. Sai, his eyes becoming round and liquid like cups full of chai, is being saying, 'Sir? Are you sure?'

Myself is not being sure of anything. The only thing that is being sure is what is happening outside. The riot makers are turning Kalyanpuri and Trilokpuri into a shamshan ghat. My wireless is hissing all the time, but I am not filing a report or going out to cover my area. I am sitting on my chair, like a haramzada without tatte. The constables are killing flies.

Myself not telling the Dilli girl, Amrit, that I am doing nothing but sitting on my fat gaand when rioting is happening in my area on first November nineteen-eighty-four. Myself only telling her that I am following orders. She is writing in her notebook. I am not looking at her mammays. I am trying not to be crying like a baby.

There are other things myself is not telling her. Like, on that day, I am hearing the sound of an engine outside the police station. I am thinking, maybe the Station House Officer is coming here to plan the counter attack. But I am seeing a truck being parked under a tree, in the police compound. The driver is getting out of the truck and walking towards me. He is also a police afsar, but from a station close by.

'Hor paaji, kiddan?' he is saying to me. I am feeling irritated by his cheerfulness. Nothing much is going on, I am feeling like answering, except a riot in my area.

'Everything is under control,' he is saying, about the situation outside. I am staring at the truck. Many flies are flying around it. I am finding it strange. The tree it is being parked under is not fruiting or flowering, and I am never seeing so many flies in one spot. I am walking towards the truck.

'Paaji, no need to go there if you don't want to. Someone will come soon and take it away,' the police afsar is saying. I am ignoring him. I am wanting to go there and be inspecting the truck. I am wanting to see why a cloud of flies, dark like the clouds in the sky before monsoon, is collecting above the truck. I am wanting to know why there is a strong smell in the police compound—it is being coming from the truck. I am walking to the back side of the truck and opening the latch. A head is rolling to the floor. I am seeing more body parts in the truck—arms, legs, faces with eyes hanging from the sockets, long and curly hair sticking to each other with blood.

Myself, sub-inspector of Kalyanpuri Police Station, is seeing my district in the bits and pieces that are lying inside the truck. I am seeing muscular arms that could be belonging to the local scooter mechanic I am knowing. I am seeing the smashed face of someone I am calling 'Chacha'. I am seeing the melted skin of the neighbourhood boys, with whom I am sometimes playing cricket in the gali. I am still seeing those body parts, all these years later. Those body parts are keeping me awake. They are demanding the rest of their bodies. They are demanding a proper cremation and last rites.

But all this, I am keeping to myself. I am not telling the Dilli girl. What if she is hearing about the body parts and fainting, or doing vomit on my charpoy?

Myself telling her that following the orders of the Station House Officer is getting me a promotion.

'Really? But according to the archived news reports, many Sikhs died…' she is touching her silver earring and talking to me.

'Arre madamji, you either be reading the old newspapers, or you be listening to me. People are dying every day. Why are you caring so much about those who are dying so many years ago,' I am saying to her. I am not telling her that those who are dying so many years ago are killing me, every day. I am not telling her that a madarchod like myself should be in jail, and not be sitting on a charpoy, sipping lassi, and growing old in this district.

Officer on Special Duty

I

Little things lifted her above the bleakness of the day. Like the layers of blue eyeshadow she wore to work—accents of teal, royal and electric blue that bestowed upon her eyelids the look of an '80s rock star. All the glamour her life could stake a claim to was concentrated in her eyelids. There were other parts of her body that also received careful aesthetic intervention, like her lips, which were always a shade of rose brown with hints of bitter chocolate. But it was her eyelids, glimmering like sapphires, which made her unique in that cramped office. They were plush canopies, fringed by mascara-heavy lashes, and she could pull these canopies down whenever her eyes revealed too much, or threatened to leak and disfigure the azure strokes that framed them.

Ruhani's eyes had read enough over the years to express anything more than mild dismay at the atrocities mentioned in the FIRs she was expected to scrutinize. But unlike the other members of the legal action committee she worked for, she, an Officer on Special Duty, felt like howling like the ten-year-old she had been when her father was killed by rioters. Her eyes would glisten whenever the words 'iron rods' or 'grievous injury' or 'dragged her husband' or 'killed brutally' sprang at her from the FIR she was holding in her hands. The other officers and legal assistants, who were all part of the team set up to reinvestigate the murder of Sikh men during what was now commonly referred to as the '84 riots, barely looked awake as they read and reread the documents, eye-witness reports, and other evidence. Thirty-two years had gone by since the Prime Minister's assassination, and several commissions had been set up to examine incidents of organized violence against the Sikhs of Delhi. But the law had lapsed—caught in a surfeit of paperwork, tangled in committees and commissions. Criminal charges against certain politicians, who had mobilized groups of men from villages around Delhi, and had supplied them with crude arms to loot and kill, had been suspended indefinitely. There was never enough evidence against those men in their spotless white kurta-pyjamas, who had chanted, 'Khoon ka badla, khoon!' and had stoked the fury of those bands of rioters and arsonists.

Blood for blood. A creed that had turned Delhi into a lunatic, frothing with rage, stalking the streets for sardars to douse in kerosene, wanting the bodies of dead men to graze a sky billowing with smoke. Blood for blood. The slogan had claimed her father too. Ramanjit Singh had been set on fire thirty-two years ago, in that crystal-and-velvet dream, Capital Residency. The curfew had just been lifted, but most of the staff had not turned up for work. He had roared at his cook, old Ravidas, for slackening in his duties, for making the few diners in his coffee shop wait longer than usual for their meal, for being an inefficient and unworthy staffer of the new hotel, his pride. He had chosen to carry a tray with glasses full of Campa Cola, from the kitchen to the coffee shop, because there was not a single waiter in the hotel on that day. They had killed him then, as he walked through the long corridor with its stained-glass mirrors. They had pinned him to the marble floor, and doused him with kerosene.

Ruhani's eyes grew moist at the memory and she drew her cerulean eyelids over them. Her family had gone to collect Ramanjit Singh's remains from the debris of the hotel—Ruhani was but a girl of ten but she had insisted on going along with the group of adults, who had received a phone call from Ravidas, incoherent because his wails had swallowed his words. Ramanjit Singh had already been reduced to ashes—all that remained of him was the steel kara he always wore on his right arm. Ruhani had walked away from the pile of charred flesh—this was not the Papaji she adored, this was not the Papaji who bought her cassettes of Wham!, Madonna, Cyndi Lauper and The Bangles, to be played again and again, on her new Sony tape deck. This was not the Papaji who wanted to take her to Italy for the summer, for a shopping expedition in search of the perfect espresso machine (they could visit the Colosseum and St Peter's Basilica too, if Ruhani felt like it).

Ruhani had wandered away from the adults, towards the dining hall, where the crystal chandelier lay in a heap of baubles—pendants, candle tubes, stem glass, top canopy, bottom bowl. She remembered now, as she sat amid a pile of FIRs, how her father used to delight in the way the crystal refracted the light in the room. 'What a sight, a rainbow inside!' he used to say. The light was strange on that day, she recalled now—it was torn to tiny bits of yellow by the broken crystal.

The family had rebuilt the hotel; it was now called Capital Grand: A Luxury 4-Star Hotel. Ramanjit Singh's brothers had taken over the business and ran it with impersonal efficiency. They could never earn the fifth star that Ramanjit Singh had longed for. Ruhani knew that was because Ravidas, the 'multi-speciality cook' had never gone back to the hotel; that Papaji's crystal rainbows were broken and could never be repaired; that Papaji himself—the heart and soul of Capital Residency—had turned to ash in the hotel that he had built.

Her cobalt eyelids were a silent homage to the blue velvet of Capital Residency. She was no longer the daughter of a prosperous hotelier; the hotel's domes and chandeliers and stained glass corridors were now a distant glimmer. Her job, as Officer on Special Duty, was a vocation her grief had responded to. She would spend her years reading about other fathers who had been killed; she would collect evidence against those men in white kurta-pyjamas; she would move the courts. And the blue eyeshadow, which she wore every day, would remind her as she pored over neatly typed reports of the carnage, that she was still alive—her anguish had kept her alive.

II

The office of the legal action committee was within the compound of Rakab Ganj Sahib gurdwara. Ruhani stood near the gurdwara's yellow gates that were framed by domed, pillared and carved gateposts. She was waiting for Nirmal Kaur. They were going to Karkardooma District Courts, to shout a variety of slogans. One of the politicians, against whom charges had been pressed for rioting and murder, had been acquitted by the courts. The women were going to protest against the verdict. Nirmal Kaur, who lived in the Widow's Colony, had been herding bereaved women and orphaned children from the colony into a Matador van every year, for the last twenty years or so. The vehicle, a tin rectangle, rattled its way to the courts, where the women staged their protest. They had, in the past, beaten their chests and shouted their laments to silent and stately buildings, hoping their cries would reach the lawmakers who sat in their chambers. They had held placards with the names of those politicians, who, with all the authority their white kurta-pyjamas and Gandhi topis bestowed upon them, had commandeered hordes of rioters across Delhi during those few days. They had demanded that the politicians be sentenced to death. Their cries had been heard by the guards stationed outside the courts, and by the crows on the neem trees, who had cawed in agreement when the women had shouted the names of the politicians, and suffixed them with an agonizing 'Hai! Hai!' The law had been deaf to their sloganeering, but these women, whose bloodlines had terminated abruptly because of the riot, had arrived every year, to rent the skies that hung over the courts with their dirges.

Today, they would challenge the verdict. There were FIRs against this politician who had been absolved of his crime. Ruhani had compiled the documents and submitted them to the new Special Investigation Team. They would break the gates of the court complex down, if that was what it took to make the lawmakers reread the FIRs. They would hand out copies of FIRs—as though the documents were flyers promoting a weight-loss programme, or a super-herb that made cancerous tumours disappear—to passers-by, so that word would spread that the acquitted man was a dangerous instigator.

Ruhani turned to gaze at the gurdwara, her hands cupping her indigo eyelids to protect them from the sun. How serene it looked in the early-evening light. Its white marble radiated with the benevolence of the ten gurus; gurbani emanated from its arched doorways, inviting the world-weary to seek divine love by surrendering to the rhythm of ancient couplets. The rioters had broken into Rakab Ganj Sahib too; Ruhani recalled reading a journalist's affidavit; it had made her wonder if the legal action committee had set up office here, within the precincts of this pale and magnificent shrine, as an act of defiance. The bastions of justice had risen from the ashes of carnage, and would fight till they were vindicated, she thought, observing the mynas that were perched on the telephone wires that ran across the sky like aerial railway tracks.

The rioters who had made their way to Rakab Ganj Sahib a day after the Prime Minister's assassination, had walked from Teen Murti Bhavan, where the slain leader's body lay in state. They had chanted 'Khoon ka badla, khoon!' along the near-empty streets and roundabouts. They had arrived at the gurdwara, swarming in through the gates, shouting their vicious slogan and impatient for blood to spill on scared ground. A formation of men from the Central Reserve Police Force stood blocking their way. The rioters slowed their advance, expecting to be attacked. But the men in uniform merely stood there, like toy soldiers that have been removed from cardboards boxes and assembled in columns for imminent combat. They stood there; they did not move—Ruhani had read the affidavit over and over again to make sense of the words.

While the platoon of policemen that had taken root at the gurdwara's grounds watched, the rioters went about their business of finding Sikh men to butcher. There were very few people in the gurdwara—the devout had disappeared into their homes the moment the first bus was set alight at the AIIMS intersection and news had spread about the possibility of more violence. So the rioters broke open the doors of the residential complex within the gurdwara's compound. They caught hold of the granthis and bhaijis there—a few of the older ones were reciting the evening banis from their gutkas, which they held with trembling hands, while the younger ones crouched under their charpoys, afraid for their lives, crying openly. One would never know how many of them were set on fire—Ruhani tried to remember if the FIR mentioned the specific number of granthis found charred within the Rakab Ganj residential complex—but there were many prayers that did not reach the Guru that evening, there were many lips that had recited the ardaas and sung kirtans in the past, which were stilled during the hour of the Rehras Sahib.

The police had watched the massacre, paralysed by what was later revealed to be the command of a politician. The journalist's affidavit mentioned a man in a white kurta-pyjama standing on the periphery of the gurdwara's grounds. When the rioters had entered the gurdwara, the man in white had raised his right hand—a quick gesture that instructed the platoon not to move. The commandos had been tranquilized by this man, who had disappeared in a white Ambassador with its red beacon light, when the rioters broke into the residence of the gurdwara's keepers.

This was the man who had been pardoned by the courts. The evidence was 'insubstantial', the verdict had stated, even though the charges against him were numerous—instigating the rioters, criminal conspiracy against the Sikhs, abetment of murder. This was the man whose name they would scream, today, outside the courts, so that it would hang in the air like an evil spirit that must be exorcised.

Ruhani could hear the 'Pom-Pom!' of the Matador's horn, as it turned towards the gurdwara's gates. She closed her blue eyelids and whispered a quick prayer—although there was every reason to believe that the Guru, like the courts, was quite deaf.

III

The Matador's engine coughed up smoke and rasped to a halt outside the gurdwara. Ruhani stepped into the tin rectangle, looking for a place to sit. Nirmal Kaur had gathered quite a crowd. Her son Satnam Pal Singh, who was the prosperous owner of a taxi stand in South Delhi, sat in front, with his thick shaggy arm around his mother. Satnam, whose father Sukhwinder had been killed in the riot, had grown up with the memory of running across the curfewed streets of this city, to a relief camp that had hurriedly been set up for Sikh women and children. Everything around them was in flames—shops, houses, scooters, men. Nirmal Kaur had made him drink his own urine, to keep him from fainting as they ran.

Gyani was there too. Ruhani knew them all, through their unique tragedies that had been scribbled on FIRs and compiled by officers like herself, to be reviewed by the committees and commissions that regrouped every few years, after long periods of sloth and indifference. Gyani had bundled her husband into a wooden cabinet with sliding doors on the day the rioters had walked into Sector 32, Trilokpuri. The cabinet also contained the family's Salora TV set, but there was enough room for one adult to hide inside it. The rioters, who had found Sikh men hiding in old steel trunks, cooking-gas cabinets, in-between the rafters that held up the ceilings of many of the tiny homes in this sector, were quick to discover Gyani's husband. One of the men lit a matchstick and threw it on the cabinet. Gyani's husband burned, with the sheesham wood of the cabinet, and the phosphor and magnetic coils and circuit board of the TV that had filled his life with monochromatic images. Did he die with the regret that he never bought his wife a Prestige Pressure Cooker, which advertised itself on TV as the only pressure cooker one bought if one loved one's wife? Or did he die with a song from *Sharaabi* on his lips?

The FIR—cold enumerator of criminal events—had omitted the details of what was on Gyani's husband's mind when he died with his black-and-white TV, thought Ruhani, as she looked at Gyani now. Life had aged the widow long before the years had left their imprint on her face. But the jaw that contoured her face was still firm, like the resilient boundaries of a ravaged kingdom. She was a survivor, this Gyani; she was an activist, this woman with the parchment face and steady jawline.

Ruhani stumbled through the narrow aisle of the Matador, half-smiling at the many faces she recognized. Here was Guneeta, who had crouched inside a giant water pipe with her three children—two boys and an infant girl, for days before someone had found her and put her in a truck on its way to a relief camp; Jasbir, whose husband, brother-in-law and old father-in-law were thrown into a bonfire of other bodies, sat by the window; Manjeet, who always brought a thermos full of tea for the protestors, sat next to Jasbir. Ruhani reached the rear of the Matador. A woman sat there, alone. A notebook lay on her lap, and she was writing on a lined page. Her silver earrings dangled as she wrote, and she pushed her wavy hair away from her face from time to time. Ruhani had never seen her before.

'Is this seat taken?' Ruhani asked the woman, pointing to the seat next to her, on which lay a black canvas bag with white owls painted on it.

'Wha…oh! Oh no, no, you can sit here…' said the woman, removing her bag from the vacant seat and dropping her notebook and pen as she put the bag on her lap.

Ruhani sat down next to the woman. The Matador's engine emitted a long metallic stammer as it started, and its wheels crunched the gravel on the road.

Ruhani stared at the woman, who had bent down to retrieve her notebook and banged her head against the seat in front of her, as she struggled to sit upright again. 'I'm Ruhani.'

'Nice to meet you,' said the woman, feeling her forehead. 'I'm Amrit.'

Ruhani felt Amrit's gaze linger on her blue eyeshadow. Was she smirking?

'So are you…you couldn't possibly be…do you live…are you a relative of one of the poor widows in this van?' Ruhani hoped she had been specific enough to elicit a clear response. She was curious about this Amrit.

'Oh, no no no! I'm a journalist…Nirmal Kaurji, whom I have met, said I could come…to observe…'

Ruhani let Amrit ramble on about her assignment. Journalists. She had met so many of them, over the years. All they really cared about was their bylines. Didn't Amrit know that this story was an old one? She should seek her byline elsewhere; Delhi was full of scoops…But why weren't they moving?

The Matador had come to a halt. One of the women—was it Gyani—said, 'Oye ki hua?'

A row of cars and scooters behind the Matador started to honk frantically. Ruhani saw Satnam roll up his sleeves and get off the van. A few of the other men—sons and nephews of the widows—followed Satnam. Ruhani peered out of the Matador's window. The men stood behind the vehicle and pushed it together.

The engine coughed dryly, then went dead.

'Dum laga ke haisha!' shouted the men, in chorus, and gave the van a mighty push.

The Matador jerked to a start. It moved ahead slowly, gathering speed as the men pushed. The engine spat dark fumes when the driver popped the clutch, and roared to life. The men ran alongside before jumping onto the footboard.

'What a dinosaur…this van…what if it hadn't started?' Amrit asked, clutching the sides of her seat as the Matador rattled ahead.

'Well…then…we would have walked all the way from Rakab Ganj to Karkardooma,' Ruhani replied, her blue canopies closing down for the rest of the journey.

EPILOGUE

Q&A

In a freewheeling interview, the assassinated Prime Minister talks about the day she died, her family, her books, and the foliage in her garden.

By Amrit Kaur

Q: Thank you for agreeing to speak with *The New Milieu* on this cold October day. Before we begin, I wanted to know… is that the same orange sari you wore, on this day, thirty-two years ago?

A: Yes, it is…it is the same sari I wore for an interview that was meant to happen in my lawns…has it really been thirty-two years? I'll take you to the spot where a journalist—a Goodwill Ambassador with the most beatific expression on his face—was waiting for me. I'll take you to the banyan tree in my lawns. We will sit, under a canopy of roots that dangle like nooses from the branches. You will ask me questions; I will answer, and you will make notes—although I don't see you carrying a notebook. The bearer will bring the tea—a golden Darjeeling or a full-bodied Assam. This time, he will bring it in the right teapot. Thirty-two years ago, he carried a teapot unworthy of the tea inside it, and of the occasion it was meant to be present at. Thirty-two years ago, I had sent the bearer back to the kitchen, and had instructed him to appear with a teapot dignified enough to appear on Irish television. The Goodwill Ambassador waited and waited, more eagerly for the tea than for me, of that I am certain, for it was a cold day, colder than it is today. Neither appeared, as you are aware; as history and its many chroniclers have stated, time and again; as the banyan and neem and rows of Ashoka trees in my lawns have witnessed. But you, Miss... hmm...what did you say your name was? You will have your tea, and your interview. We will sip the tea, and your cameras will record the meeting...but...I don't see any cameras either. Are you sure you have come prepared for this interview...hmm Miss...aahaa!...Miss...Ankita? Miss Anita? The Goodwill Ambassador brought an entire crew of people along, and his giant cameras nearly destroyed my rows of poppies and dahlias. I heard about the little murders that took place in my lawns—saplings mangled by cables, sunflowers beheaded by careless hands trying to arrange the equipment—as I sat in front of my dressing table, getting my hair done. But, you haven't brought any equipment my dear...aaahhaa!...my dear girl, how do you intend to interview me?

Q: Amrit, Madam Prime Minister, Madam Late Prime Minister, my name is Amrit. And this device here—my smartphone—will perform all the functions of notebooks and gigantic cameras and tape recorders. Also, it's a compact device, as you can see, so it will not cause any damage to the plants and trees of your lawns. But tell me, how have you spent your time, for the thirty-two years that you have been dead?

A: Well, dear Amrit, I haven't given any interviews since my assassination, nor have I spoken with the press that visits this bungalow, every now and then, to take photographs of my living room, my study, my bedroom. My personal belongings—the orange sari I am wearing today, another sari that lies folded on a stool in my bedroom, the conch and rosary in my prayer room, my medals, the photographs of my children and grandchildren, the black telephone in my study—are now called *artefacts,* and are there for all to see. My home is a museum; the private moments I spent in it are on display for throngs of tourists and school children. Sometimes, I turn into a long shadow that jumps across the walls of this museum and rolls on the grass outside, hoping that a tourist will follow me to the spot where I fell, and let me narrate the facts of my death, instead of listening to a feeble voice inside what the crowd refers to as headphones (I stole a pair once, in the guise of a rhesus monkey; I bared my teeth at a young boy in school uniform and he dropped his headphones, which I grabbed and put on my head. The voice inside was scratchy and dull; its story a monotonous drone of historical events in chronological order). Sometimes, I hang upside-down with the bats in the banyan tree. When I feel nostalgic for days of long rallies and longer election discourses, I make speeches to the langurs and lilies and swallowtail butterflies here. My republic has been reduced to a crowd of jamun, jackfruit, neem, oak, alstonia and banyan trees.

But you, who have walked into my republic with your smartphone and many questions, have wiped out thirty-two years of silence. I rushed the winds to meet you—did you feel a sudden gust as you entered the pillared doorway? I stopped a peacock in mid-dance and instructed the bird to fly me here, to you. It would amuse me to talk to your smartphone—I observed you speaking to it from a branch on the old banyan, where I was picking berries to garnish a meal of dead sparrows and bat droppings.

Q: The smartphone is recording you as you speak, Madam Late Prime Minister. Before we walk to the banyan tree in the lawns, let us walk around your home, this memorial. Let us dwell on a few of the exhibits, for instance, the orange hand-spun sari with its black border…the one you are wearing today. It has been preserved here for all these years, for generations to stare at your bloodstains, to take photographs of the holes made on the fabric by the bullets you received. Your black sandals lie with it, together with the red cloth bag with its woven pattern that you carried on that day. What were your final thoughts before the bullets pierced your sari?

A: My final thoughts? Well, you know, I had several thoughts on that day—I was so preoccupied as I walked down my garden path, and obviously, I didn't know that those thoughts would be my final. There was a dinner party I was hosting later that evening, for a visiting princess. As you probably know—and if you don't, the placard outside my dining room will inform you—I prepared for luncheons and dinners with the same attentiveness with which I prepared for election rallies, speeches in Parliament, special operations and coups. The silverware had to be polished so that it reflected the face of the dignitary, official or friend, or even troublesome faction, while holding a desert spoon or speaking across a candle stand. The crockery had to have the most delicately expressive patterns; the napkins had to be folded with a symmetry matched only by the contours of the Taj Mahal.

I was pleased with my hairstyle on that day; it calmed me to feel that my hair looked good, even though arrangements for the dinner were still underway and I worried that we might not be prepared to receive the princess on time. Also, I was tired. I had returned from a pre-election rally the previous night—the Goodwill Ambassador had flown with me—he had wanted to hear me address the farmers, small traders and their wives who had walked miles from their villages to the rally grounds, just to hear me speak. I was tired; I'm sure the Goodwill Ambassador was tired; I was keen to wrap up the interview and perhaps take a nap before getting involved with the preparations for the night.

The day ended abruptly—as we all know. My bodyguards sprayed me with bullets—as we all know. One shot at me from a .38 service revolver, while the other used a Sten gun. Those are the facts; they have been documented innumerable times and I hope your generation, with its equipment-free methods of interviewing heads-of-state (even dead ones) is not ignorant of the details of my assassination. No no, there is no need to smile sheepishly…I am sure your smartphone is doing a competent job of recording me.

As I was saying, my bodyguards shot me on the garden path that links this residence to my office…and I will take you there. It was a favourite path, fringed with a Putranjiva hedge. Bamboo stalks formed a tender canopy over me, as I walked towards the banyan tree, where the Goodwill Ambassador was waiting with his camera crew. Elephant Palms stood in semi circles; in the lawns beyond I could see the fleshy white blooms of the Malta trees. A row of Ashoka trees that had recently been pruned caught my attention, the leaves looked so glossy and new, and then…and then…they shot at me, quick shots from the revolver followed by the long metallic rasping from the Sten gun. I fell; the Ashoka trees seemed unmoved by this violent turn of events; I found myself thinking, as my face hit the gravel path, that the Ashoka has many, many names. In Sanskrit, it is called Anganapriya, Ashopalava, Asupala. Ashoka means *sorrow-less*. Those, Miss…aah…Amrit, were my last thoughts, before the lawns grew dark.

Q: Interesting, Madam Late Prime Minister, that in your final moments, you were preoccupied with the etymology of the word Ashoka. You loved words, didn't you? And books? Which were your favourite?

A: Which were my favourite words, or books? You should be more specific, Miss Amrit, but I'll spare you the trouble of rephrasing your question, and speak of both. There were words like Popocatepetl that I loved; words like Chimborazo fascinated me; I was interested in philology (still am, if you're willing to believe that the dead can pursue linguistics), and the sound and texture of certain words. Among the many books in my study here are titles like *1001 Ways to Improve Your Conversation and Speeches*, a most helpful guide, and *The Faber Book of Aphorisms*. There are books on history and politics, displayed here—see that leather-bound and gold embossed *Stories From French History?* It stands next to *The French Revolution: a History. In Three Volumes*—pompous volumes, I dare say, and appropriate as exhibits here, but not my favourite. There were books that were gifted to me by my American friend Dorothy, her own *The Heroic Encounter*, and William Irwin Thompson's *At The Edge of History* (which was incomprehensible in parts, I have to admit). I found solace in Tagore, and strength in Karl Marx. Dylan Thomas' radio drama, *Under Milk Wood* saw me through the early years of leading my political party, when I was prone to frequent bouts of fainting…thought I'd mention it even though it's not a book! I was enthralled, I must confess, by *The Third Eye*—have you heard of it? It was written by one Tuesday Lobsang Rampa, who was actually an English plumber who claimed that he had been possessed by a Tibetan lama. Does the occult interest you, Miss Amrit? Does the afterlife?

Q: Not really, Madam Late Prime Minister, I have very little knowledge of such things. And, for the purpose of our readers (some of whom were born in the decades after you were assassinated), I request you to focus on the more earthly details of the exhibits here. Which of them were you particularly attached to, or held a special significance in your life?

A: You really should have come prepared with a more comprehensive set of questions, Miss Amrit, rather than repeating the same old *Which is your favourite this* and *Which is your favourite that!* But let me indulge you, for who knows how many decades, or even centuries will go by, before another journalist arrives here, seeking me.

My childhood, my marriage, the tumult of my political career…all of it is here, in these objects of daily use, in these rooms, in these lawns. These displays are relics of love, of family, of friends from all over the world. Here is a framed photograph of Rabindranath Tagore, and a handwritten *Where The Mind Is Without Fear*, which I kept in my study. Here is a wooden box with carvings as delicate as lace, which my husband made for me. We met when I was thirteen, and he, eighteen. Did you know that he proposed to me on the steps of the Basilica of Sacré-Coeur in the young and giddy Paris of 1937? Memories are trapped here, Miss Amrit, but you, like everyone else, choose to call them *exhibits*.

Over there…let us walk to that section…are gifts from world leaders and revolutionaries. See that lead crystal Dome of the Rock? It was from the Palestinian people. And that lacquer plate with Ho Chi Minh smiling at us? The government of Vietnam presented me with it. There are keys to the cities of Bogota, Port of Spain, Washington—have you ever held a ceremonial key in the palm of your hand, Miss Amrit? Entire cities whisper their secrets to you, want to reveal their treasures to you, want to tell you of terrors and thrills and things feverishly prayed for.

My favourite people are here too. My father is here, sitting on a grassy slope, with my sons, children then. My mother is here; her face covered by her sari pallu in that sepia portrait. That's me, when I was five, holding a British doll close to my chest (I later threw that doll into a bonfire of other British goods). That's me again, with my grown-up sons in Paris, in 1966. Those are my sons, carrying an urn with my father's ashes, in Allahabad. We are all alive, Miss Amrit, we exhibits are alive! Why not wait until dusk to interview us all, with your smartphone. When the evening gathers around Lutyens' Delhi and the crowd retreats from my residence and fades into its many ordinary lives, when the raat-ki-rani maddens the cicadas with its perfume and makes them moan, that is when we emerge—dead fathers and mothers and sons. At the hour of the bat, we stir; at the hour of the eel, we step out of the glass displays that trap us; at the hour of the ghost, we become family once again, untouched by assassination, innocent of murder. Our clothes are no longer blood-stained or bullet-riddled or torn to shreds in a bomb blast—our clothes are new and whole, like the orange sari I am wearing now…I am alive, Miss Am…

Q: Madam Late Prime Minister, sorry to interrupt you, but we have reached the garden path. It is covered in crystal, and is meant to look like a flowing river. This glass slab here, with a quote by you on it, has been placed on the spot where you fell. How do you feel about this shimmering memorial; is it a fitting tribute to you, to your spirit?

A: Miss Amrit, let me respond to your question with a question. Do you really believe that a slab of glass is suitable homage to my *spirit*, even if it is engraved with my writings? You make me laugh, Miss Amrit, and not because I'm amused.

Look around you, Miss Amrit, look at my sorrow-less Ashoka; observe my Elephant Palms that are almost vulgar in their health and beauty; feel the texture of my Kadam trees that ooze sapwood; smell the soft musk of my Bael trees, swollen with fruit and shrouded in beehives. My garden thrives, even though it witnessed my murder, Miss Amrit, it flowers and bears fruit as it is meant to with the change of the seasons. My garden is unaltered by tragedy, Miss Amrit; these trees are the *fitting homage* you mentioned; the rest is merely for the amusement of the busloads of tourists who arrive here.

And the banyan—we have finally reached the old banyan—is where I have waited, all these years, to be interviewed. Come then, Miss Amrit, let us sit under its grand shade, or, would you rather sit on a branch? I could lift you up, to the topmost branch, my favourite perch. From there, we could speak of many things—past difficulties as Prime Minister of this country, and present difficulties as overseer of this republic of langurs, reptiles and winged creatures. Nothing much has changed, really.

Acknowledgements

This book is the result of a last-minute bid to get into the University of East Anglia's (UEA) first creative writing workshop in India, held in Kolkata in 2013. A short story read and critiqued by a group of very bright people became the scaffolding for this enthusiastic but amateurish production. I am grateful to Amit Chaudhuri, who presided over the workshop, for his encouragement, his gentle evaluation and comments, his intellect—always formidable and never flashy.

Thanks are also due to Romesh Gunesekera, co-tutor of the first workshop, for warm conversation, and for making me feel like I was already the author I was trying to become.

At the UEA, I am indebted to Henry Sutton, for his interest in the collection, and his eagle-eyed intervention.

Speaking Tiger Books is just the publisher an unknown voice could hope for—unafraid of newness, willing to flout mainstream parameters and conventional wisdom to take on a novel-told-in-short-stories type of debut. Many thanks are due to Ravi Singh, for his faith in this structural oddity, for coffee and a speedy signing of my first contract. I am also deeply grateful to Anurag Basnet, for his matter-of-factness, his editorial wisdom, his quiet collaboration.

Ultimately, had it not been for my friends and family, I would have remained the snivelling baby that I believe I no longer am. For that, and for being a highly-intelligent first reader, I am grateful to Sabu Paul. Thanks are also due to Prithvishwar Gayen, for his patience, his early cover designs, his careful reading.

And then there is Seraphin Zimik, with her rare gift of unconditional friendship. There is Manav Kumar, with whom I spent the best of my youth. Finally, and most importantly, there are Surist and Jyotika—my father and sister—the very centre of my life, whose tough love has seen me through.